Books by S. Kodejs

Better Off Dead (The Spirit Seeker Series)

Eternity (Eternity Series)

The Manitou, Book One

The Manitou, Book Two

Dance For The Devil

For auntie Qi!
I am so blessed to have
you in my life! You are
the best aunt ever + have
always supported me from
the very first ☺
♡ Shan

THE SPIRIT SEEKER SOCIETY

A Ghost Story

Dedicated with love

To the fabulous Kodejs Men

Dave, Tanner, Shawn & Chase

CHAPTER ONE

'If I cannot move Heaven, I will raise Hell' – Virgil

The assignment was simple. First year students at the University of King's College were required to create a *'society'*. Groups of four to five students were randomly assigned, selected by the Dean as he drew names from an old-fashioned top hat. All subject matters were allowed, but the proposal had to meet certain requirements. The society needed to be of a historical, philanthropic, community, or arts-based agenda. Bonus marks were given for originality, and the groups would meet throughout the term. A murmur rolled through the two-hundred-plus members in the theater-style auditorium. The students were not anticipating this as there'd been no precedent – yes, the existing societies at King's were steeped in tradition and every year, a handful of new ones popped up like tulip bulbs. They ranged from the sublime – *The King's Concert Collective*, to the whimsical – *The Philosophy and Baking Club*, to the purely recreational – *The Gaming Society*. While enrollment in a society was encouraged, it had never been mandatory, so the students were caught off guard. Some embraced it, others were less enthusiastic and an uncomfortable fidgeting rippled through the auditorium. They'd heard stories of how challenging the Foundation Year Program was and this unexpected element could prove detrimental.

"The benefit," the Dean elaborated, ignoring their mumblings, "is immeasurable. King's College has been referred to as 'Harvard of the North'. All universities have intelligent graduates. King's graduates are more than just book smart: they are innovators, community leaders, and above all, thinkers. When you graduate in four years time, you no will longer be ordinary. You will be *kings*."

**

Nora Berkowitz studied her fellow society members with disdain. Without exception, they were attractive. *No*, she corrected herself, *she was the exception.* To be fair, the Middle Eastern boy was merely average looking but Nora suspected with a proper haircut, better clothing, and the disposal of his eighties-style, clunky eyeglasses, he'd go from a five to an eight. The bone structure was there, and there was something exotically beautiful about his dark, heavily fringed large eyes and British-Indo accent. He had just introduced himself: Ashwin Pawar from Pondicherry, India.

"I am nineteen," Ashwin was saying, "and I intend to pursue a degree in Biochemistry and Molecular Biology. You may wonder why I am enrolled in the Foundation Year, if that is to be my field of study. My father felt it essential to improve my knowledge of classical literature. His exact sentiment was: *'Anyone can be a scientist, Ashwin, but you must be well-versed in the social sciences as well.'* To that end, I also play field hockey like all good Indian boys, although I must confess, I do not play it well."

The group chuckled and Nora frowned. *Great. He was charming as well as potentially attractive.* She would have no allies in this group.

"Hi, I'm Maggie Bench," said the only other female member of the group, with a little hand flourish. She was stunningly pretty with blond hair that fell in ringlets halfway down her back, which, unlike Nora's, did not look inclined to frizz. "I'm local

8

– from Halifax, but my parents insisted I live in rez so I can get the full university experience." She sighed softly, and Nora noticed all eyes were riveted on her. Petite, tanned, toned, dressed in a simple flowered sundress, Maggie Bench looked like every girl that ever graced a magazine cover. Nora hated her on sight. "I'll be honest. King's wasn't my first choice. I wanted to study abroad. I yearn to get out of the proverbial fishbowl but my folks insisted I complete the FYP year first, and then they'll pay for wherever I choose. I'm thinking England, maybe, or France. I don't know, haven't decided. I wanted to take a gap year, see the world, but my folks insisted I turn nineteen first. The minute this year is up, I'm heading to Thailand, Vietnam... Nepal. That's the real way to learn, you know. Education will only get you so far, you need to *experience* life."

Heads around the table bobbed in agreement, and annoyingly, Nora found herself joining in. Maggie Bench was mesmerizing. As she nodded, Nora pictured a giant pitchfork falling from the ceiling and impaling Maggie Bench's perfect blond curls.

"Yo, what's up? I'm Alec Yeats, I'm almost eighteen. I agree with Maggie, I think school is lame but my folks insisted. They went to King's. They're journalists for the Chronicle Herald and they think I should be too, but writing is so not my thing. I play football, defensive-back. I wanted to play university ball but I'm too small for the top schools. I'm trying out for the Dalhousie team, though. They compete in the Atlantic Football League. Not CIS, but..." he shrugged, "it's still football, right? You can play for Dalhousie if you go to King's. That was the only reason I agreed to enroll. I have no idea what my major is going to be, maybe Marine Biology or

Oceanography because the beach is cool. Or maybe not, I think you have to be good in science for that. Maybe Law? Yeah, I totally can see being a cop." Alec held his fingers up in a mock shooting and pretended to blast away the windows. He was stocky and on the short side, perhaps five-eight. He had dark, cropped hair that was vaguely militant, and his upper arm sported a barbed-wired tattoo. "Hey, Ash, you said you're nineteen? Sweet, you can legally buy booze."

Ashwin looked alarmed. "I don't drink."

"Hey, man, this is university. *Everyone* drinks. It's gonna be a year-long party." He smiled at everyone, focusing in particular on Maggie. "Am I right?"

"How on earth did you get accepted?" Nora blurted. "I mean, admission standards are rigorous at King's, and no offence, but you seem like a dumb jock."

Alec frowned. "I'm gonna take that as a compliment, because it means I'm not a nerd." He looked at Nora as if noticing her for the first time and Nora flinched. It was always that way: people glossed over her like she didn't exist. You'd think her size alone would make her stand out – but no, she was the six-foot-elephant in the room. Unusually tall for a woman, with a shock of frizzy dark hair that she swept forward to better hide her face. Nora had a Jewish nose and small, close-set grey eyes that took in everything. Her skin was beyond fair – it burnt at the slightest chance and had the unfortunate habit of turning lobster-red at the smallest provocation. On the plus side, her acne had finally cleared up thanks to a three month stint of Accutane and her teeth were straight, compliments of her orthodontist uncle. Regardless of the clear skin and nice teeth – last week a little boy pointed at her in the grocery and asked his mother if Nora was a witch.

"Nora, where are you from?" Daniel O'Shea asked. He was the final member of the group and Nora had purposely avoided looking at him. Daniel O'Shea was the male equivalent of Maggie Bench, perfect with tousled light brown hair, ripped body and suntanned skin. Exquisite bone-structure with high, angular cheek bones and a perfect, narrow nose. His clothes were simple – faded denims and a white v-neck tee, short-sleeved to show off his muscled arms. The look was timeless: it looked as hot today as it did fifty years ago on James Dean. When he smiled at her, Nora swore the lights in the room dimmed. Maybe it was the way he smelled: like lemons. She could smell him all the way across the table and the scent was tantalizing. Or, perhaps it was his accent: a slight lilt that made Nora's knees go weak and her belly feel watery. No one that pretty should be allowed to exist.

"I'm from Truro," Nora said, defiantly. "I could commute but I've chosen to live on campus. I don't want to miss any classes, especially in the winter when roads are bad." Nora did not list her age as the others had. She did not want to admit she was twenty-four. "I plan to major in Gender and Women's studies..." She broke off as she saw their expressions. No one ever considered that a viable major and it pissed her off. "Look," she said, a little harsher than intended, "I'm a serious student; I'm not here to make friends. Can we get right down to it? Does anyone have any decent ideas for a society?"

"I propose we make a society promoting healthy foods," Maggie suggested. "I mean, have you seen the cafeteria yet? The salad bar is tiny and the rest is pizza, pasta and deli meats. There's not even an organic section."

"Screw that," Alec said. "We should do something athletic and fun. Like, the Beer-Pong Society... what?" he asked, looking around the table. "It would be fun. I rock at beer-pong."

"While that does sound enjoyable," Daniel O'Shea said, "I believe we need to choose something that will better fit the guidelines. What do you think, Nora? It seems like you might have some clever ideas."

Nora slouched in her chair. Everyone was looking at her and it made her feel uncomfortable. The room was humid and she felt sweat beading under her armpits. She could smell it too; no matter how many times per day she showered and how much antiperspirant she applied, she could always smell a faint, skunky scent. "We could do an outreach of the Elizabeth Fry Society."

"What's that?" Alec asked.

"Helps women navigate the justice system."

They groaned in unison, even Maggie. Daniel was the only one who didn't chime in. "It's a great cause," he agreed, nodding at Nora, "but it doesn't meet the mandate of being an original society. We need to think outside the box, something unique to Nova Scotia, something that takes into account its rich historical past."

"How about forming *The Pier 21 Society*?" Ashwin suggested. "Pier 21 was the gateway to the new world. Over a million souls passed through its gates."

"Souls," Daniel snapped his finger. "You're onto something, Ashwin. All those people, all their stories... Why did they come, what happened to them?"

"It's not like we can ask them," Alec scoffed. "Dude, they're dead."

"Ghosts," Maggie Bench said, absently twirling a ringlet. "The Society of Halifax Ghosts."

"Ghosts don't exist," Nora said.

"Sure they do," Maggie said. "This city is filled with ghost stories. Did you know there are ghosts right here, at King's? I went on the ghost tour, in frosh week. It was awesome, totally spooky."

Nora snorted. "Ghosts of students past?"

Ashwin cleared his throat. "It's actually a workable idea. I believe that it would satisfy the criteria – an original idea with a historical theme. We could research places that are reported to be haunted, and see if we can link them to real people."

"It would be fun," Maggie continued, growing excited. "We can do a séance, get a medium."

Nora raised her eyes to the ceiling. Like many antiquated buildings, the walls were made of stone and the ceilings were vaulted. The idea was stupid. She didn't like working in groups.

"Maggie's right, it *would* be fun," Daniel said. "Everyone could choose which ghost they'd like to research and ultimately try to contact. Nora, perhaps you could find someone who was an early advocate for women's rights, someone like Edith Archibald, the suffragist."

Nora's eyes flew to Daniel. "You know about her?"

"Sure," he said easily. "You'd be just the person to bring her to life."

"Interesting choice of words."

Daniel laughed and Nora noticed the lemon scent again. She squirmed in her seat – the scent was acting like an aphrodisiac. *Was she the only one affected?*

"Let's get real, people," Daniel said, nodding at Nora. "Nora's right: there are no such things as ghosts, although there is a plethora of circumstantial evidence and folklore. But it would be a fun assignment, and easy enough that we could concentrate on our real studies. So, what do you say, group? Should we take a vote on it? Let's make it formal. I, Daniel O'Shea, submit to my fellow members that we form *The Spirit Seeker Society.* All in favor?"

The vote was unanimous. Even Nora raised her hand half-heartedly when it became apparent the majority was about to rule. It didn't hurt that Daniel looked at her directly and winked. Nora flushed, the red staining her neck and cheeks. When Daniel winked it was like Heaven opened up and God smiled directly at her.

"Okay, it's settled. Let's take a break, grab some lunch, and meet back here tonight to draw up the proposal. Start thinking about who you'd like to resurrect." Daniel struck an imaginary gavel and proclaimed the meeting adjourned.

**

The University of King's College was a small liberal arts school that occupied a corner of Dalhousie University in Halifax, Nova Scotia. Although separate institutions, they shared more than just campus space, and students were allowed to use the facilities of either campus and intermingle their courses. The first year at King's was unique – an intensive classical literature program referred to as the Foundation Year Programme, or FYP as the students called it. FYP was also an acronym for *'Forget Your Personal Life'* – because of the heavy workload. Successful students would be doing little else but studying.

Those who didn't study would find themselves politely ejected after the first term. The curriculum was rigorous, revolving around ancient texts, philosophy, history and politics. A single week might explore Dante's Inferno, The Prince, The Communist Manifesto, and the Art of War. Students would be immersed in Plato, Darwin, Descartes, Freud and Nietzsche, among others. Their literary journey would take them from the *Ancient World*, through the *Middle Ages*, touch on *The Renaissance*, and linger in the *Age of Reason* before finally ending the year in the *Contemporary World*.

Beyond receiving a superlative education, King's students could boast they belonged to the oldest university in the commonwealth outside the United Kingdom. King's was founded in 1789 and was the first English-speaking University in Canada. In a modern world eschewing formal traditions, King's held onto many of theirs. The student societies had thrived for two hundred years. Once a month, students and faculty dressed in robes and attended *Formal Meal*, and the dark, stone halls of King's looked more Hogwarts than Halifax.

King's was comprised of a series of buildings overlooking a square courtyard known as the *Quad*, a lovely little green space with flowers and pathways. Prince Hall stood on one end, holding classrooms, offices and dining areas. It housed two of the dorms while the bulk of the residences flanked the sides. In one corner stood a charming chapel while the gymnasium rounded out the other. At the far end was the library, which had a classical column facade that provided an excellent stage for both planned and impromptu concerts and theatrical displays. Throughout the entire structure, underground paths and tunnels linked so students could traverse from one building to the next without ever going outdoors. They were dark and creepy and generally showed the age of buildings long past their bicentennial, and the students tended to avoid them on all but the bitterest of days.

But cold weather was months away, and the early September sunshine was sultry. Students lounged around the Quad, eating Subway and throwing Frisbees, or just soaking up the sun while they made plans about which bar to frequent that night. In the Quad, all dreams were possible.

Alec saw Ashwin and called over, "Hey, Dude, wait up." He'd been talking to a trio of sunbathing girls and it was hard to tell if they were interested or annoyed. He thought the brunette on the end was appropriately flirty. The other two were probably closet lesbians, an opinion reinforced when the blond one ordered him to move along, that he was blocking her sun.

"Hello, Alec, isn't it?" Ashwin inquired politely.

"Yeah. I was thinking of heading to the gym to check out their free weights, wanna tag along?"

Ashwin halted and blinked. Did he? Not really. But it would be considered friendly to accept. "Sounds splendid," he said, forcing himself to speak in a partial sentence and thus blend in. Canadians were masters at casual language and he was trying his best to assimilate. Although there was an ethnic mix on campus, King's was predominately Caucasian, and Ashwin had never been more self-conscious of his brown skin. He wondered, for the hundredth time, if it would have been better to simply enrol at Dalhousie, where the racial mix was more equitable.

But Papa had been adamant for reasons that were not entirely clear to Ashwin.

"I work out every day," Alec stated. "The Dalhousie gym is bigger and better, but I thought I'd see what we have here. When the weather's bad, I might not feel like walking to the other one."

They entered the gym. Wooden floors; a small smattering of fitness equipment. "This sucks," Alec commented, frowning. They were the only ones there. "Final cuts to the football team are made tonight. There are a lot of guys trying out for my position and the coach wasn't impressed with my size. I'm gonna have to bulk up if I'm ever going to play again. So different from high school. I was a star in high school. Here I'm... nothing."

"Perhaps you could join one of the intramural teams," Ashwin suggested.

"Like what?"

Ashwin considered. "I saw a list in the Wardroom. Why don't we walk over there and check it out?"

They crossed the Quad. Alec waved to the trio of girls he'd been talking to minutes earlier and they ignored him. Even the flirty brunette. That clinched it – definitely dykes. They entered the Wardroom, a student lounge by day and campus bar by night.

"There you go, flag football," Ashwin said, pointing.

"Not really the same thing," Alec stated, and then shrugged. "But what the hell, it might be fun. Hey, they have ball hockey. Isn't that your sport?"

"I play field hockey."

"Same thing, only you do it in a gym and the stick blade is straighter."

Ashwin looked doubtful. "I suppose."

"Hey, let's make a deal – why don't we join both teams?"

"I don't know the first thing about football. And it's... violent."

"Not flag football. It's non-contact. It'll be a blast, and what better way to pick up Canadian culture than to sign up for football and hockey?"

Ashwin thought of his father's advice to assimilate. "Alright." He inked his name on both lists before he could change his mind.

"Cool, dude. Let's see if Daniel will join, too. Then *The Spirit Seeker Society* can be an official ass-kicking force."

Ashwin's eyes widened with alarm. "I thought it was non-contact?"

"In theory, yes," Alec grinned. "But not the way I play."

**

Maggie was picking through the salad bar when Nora spotted her from across the cafeteria. Two young males were moon-dogging Maggie but the pretty blond didn't appear to notice. *Figures*, thought Nora sourly. Girls like Maggie were so used to being the center of attention that those two buffoons didn't even appear on her radar.

Nora made a move to duck behind a pillar but Maggie looked up, catching her eye. *Great, now it looks like I've been staring at her,* Nora thought.

"Hey, Nora," Maggie called, completely unabashed about hollering across the crowded cafeteria. "Save me a seat." Maggie floated over with the natural grace of a dancer and took a vacant seat across from Nora. The table was on the far side of the cafeteria and was mostly empty. "Great," Maggie breathed. "I'm so happy to see a friendly face. Ugh, I don't know if I'm going to be able to survive this food. They have very little vegan selection. I will have to talk to someone about that."

"Is that all you're eating? Just a bit of lettuce and fruit?" Nora looked at her own plate. It was overflowing with a cheeseburger and fries.

"I'm not sure what's been cooked with animal products," Maggie said. She pointed at Nora's fries. "Like those – for example. A lot of times they're fried in beef fat."

"So?"

Maggie's mouth quirked. "Kind of defeats the purpose, don't you think? I'll make an appointment to speak with the school president and see what we can do about getting some vegan alternatives. I can't be the only healthy eater on campus."

Nora looked around, glancing at the other students' plates. "I wouldn't bet on that."

"They just need choices."

"So you think that'll work? You can just go in and request a menu change and they'll revamp it for you?"

"Sure. Why not?"

Nora gaped. The girl was serious. Is that how things worked in Maggie Bench's pretty little world? She simply asked for whatever she wanted and everyone accommodated? Not bloody likely. This piece of fluff needed to learn what the real world was like. This was university. No one was going to fulfill a vapid, outlandish request, no matter how lovely the purveyor was. "This I'd like to see."

"Okay, why don't we head over after lunch? That would be awesome if you'll come with me – nice to have some support."

Nora smirked and Maggie took it for a smile.

"I've been thinking about the ghost thing," Maggie said, abruptly changing the topic. "I'm going to search for the spirit of someone who died in the Halifax Explosion. Two thousand people perished – that must've generated some ghost activity."

Nora frowned. That was actually a good idea; very creative.

"What about you?" Maggie asked. "Any ideas?"

Nora looked at her fries. They seemed entirely unappealing at the moment. "I haven't given it much thought. I mean, it's a waste of time. The work load is going to be tough enough without that nonsense piled on top."

"That's the point," Maggie said, impulsively reaching for the other girl's hand. Nora recoiled as if snake bitten but Maggie appeared not to notice. "We're supposed to have fun as well, to immerse ourselves, to make connections that will last us for life. Would you like me to help you think of something? How about the Titanic?"

Damn. That was another good idea. "No, the Titanic is boring. It's been done to death."

"Ha, funny." Maggie grinned.

Nora glared and thinned her lips.

"I mean, good pun: *'Done to death'*. You have a good sense of humor, Nora. But you're right; the Titanic is over-exposed. Hey, what about –"

"Pier 21," Nora blurted. "I'm going to get my ghost from Pier 21."

"I was going to suggest –"

Nora cut her off. "Look, I don't care what you were going to suggest. I'm smart, got that? I can come up with my own ghostly breeding grounds."

"Sorry, I didn't mean to offend you. I just thought–"

Nora snorted. Although she'd been famished, her appetite vanished. Her burger and fries no longer seemed appealing. She stared at Maggie's fruit plate and the strawberries looked lush and inviting. "I can think for myself, Blondie. If I needed a cheerleader, I would have gone to a football game. I'm here to learn – not to make BFF's."

"Yeah, that is kind of high-schoolish, isn't it?" Maggie agreed, not looking the least bit offended. "Okay, I'm done. Shall we see the president now about changing the menu?" She smiled sweetly and her smile lit up the room.

Nora scowled. The girl was like baby chick. You wanted to squish the damn thing but you couldn't. She just kept bouncing back.

A good-looking guy approached and cleared his throat. "Are you done with your tray?" he asked Maggie. "I'll take it for you, save you the hassle."

"Sure," Maggie said, turning away from Nora and giving him her full attention.

"You're Maggie, right?" he asked and Maggie nodded. "I'm Kevin. I saw you in the auditorium this morning. Pretty dress, by the way, you look smokin' hot. Hey, want to meet up later in the Wardroom? There'll be dancing."

"Sure," Maggie said.

When she turned back, Nora was gone. Nora hadn't bothered to clear her tray, just left it on the table. That was against the rules. Maggie picked up the tray and took it over to the sanitation station while Kevin carried hers.

**

Nora almost ran into Daniel. She'd been fuming so hard she wasn't watching where she was going.

"Careful," he laughed, jumping back. "Man, if looks could kill, I'd be a dead man."

"Sorry." Nora had the grace to look embarrassed.

"Where you headed in such a hurry?"

Nora shrugged. "Nowhere. I was just going back to my room to study."

"Ah, studying on the first day. What a keener. We didn't even get homework."

"Thought I'd read ahead. We'll get slammed tomorrow, you know. They're just letting us acclimate for the first day."

"You're very serious, I like that about you."

"I'm paying a lot of money to be here. It's coming out of my own pocket, not Mommy and Daddy's like most of these freaks."

Daniel nodded. "May I walk you?"

"Why?" She narrowed her eyes, waiting for the punch line.

"Why not? You're very interesting."
She looked at him. "I doubt I'm your type."

Daniel smiled and ran his fingers through his wavy hair, tousling it to perfection. "I don't have a type. And besides, I'm just asking to walk with you, not marry you. But hey, if you'd rather not, I understand."

"Everyone has a type."

"Is that so? Hmm, if I had to choose, I prefer the dark-haired ladies. They're mysterious, elusive."

"Don't you have a girlfriend?"

Daniel's smile faltered slightly. "I did. But... it's complicated."

They were walking, Nora hadn't even realized. Daniel was leading her to a stairwell. "Wait, where are we going?"

"This goes to the underground passageway to Alexandra Hall. That's your dorm, isn't it?"

She frowned. "How did you know?"

"I didn't figure you for the coed dorms."

"What's that supposed to mean?"

Daniel laughed. "Nothing. Are you always this bristly? You strike me as a serious student, very smart. Not the vapid party-girl type who only wants to get her drink on. Now, do you want me to show you the tunnel or are you too afraid that I'm going to overpower you, ravish you and stuff your dead body down the garbage chute?"

Nora drew herself to her full six-foot-height. "Not worried, buster. If you tried to ravish me, it'd be your dead body stuffed down the garbage chute." But she smiled a little and relaxed.

The underground pathway was desolate. Exposed ductwork and metal pipes crisscrossed the ceilings and walls. At one time, many years ago, the walls had been painted industrial grey but the paint chipped off in large segments. Someone had made an attempt to brighten the walls with campus posters, others added graffiti. The effect was ghetto. Overall, the air was stale and the slight smell of urine emanated from the dank corners.

"This is creepy," Nora said. "I don't think I'd want to be down here by myself. It's so isolated; no one could hear you scream."

"Ah, it's not too bad," Daniel said. "It has character. Hasn't changed in over a hundred years – and just wait until it rains or the weather turns cold. Then it's packed down here."

"How would you know?" Nora asked. "Isn't this your first year?"

Daniel shrugged and smiled. "I've talked to some fourth years. And it stands to reason." As he spoke, the fluorescent lights flickered erratically, plunging them into darkness for the barest of instances until struggling to come back to life. "See, you've insulted it," Daniel joked.

Nora smiled hesitatingly. At twenty-four, this was the first time she'd really talked to a boy who wasn't her cousin. It was very nice.

So, why then, were alarm bells ringing in her head and shivers coursing down her spine? She fought the urge to bolt. She was such a loser, always uncomfortable around men. Certainly one as attractive as Daniel. "You know," she said, only half joking, "this would be the perfect spot to search for ghosts."

The lights flickered again, plunging them into complete darkness.

CHAPTER TWO

*'Some things you will think of yourself...some things
God will put into your mind' – Homer*

"Maybe Maggie isn't coming?" Ashwin suggested. The other four members of the newly formed Spirit Seeker Society were gathered in a small meeting room on the second floor of Prince Hall.

"I did say eight," Daniel said, frowning. "It's a quarter past now."

"I'm not surprised," Nora said acridly. "Maggie Bench doesn't strike me as the type who cares enough about other people to be on time."

"Should we start without her?" Alec wondered, looking out the window. "They're posting the final roster for the football team at nine and I want to be there. Why don't we start without her?"

Daniel paced. "It's our first meeting and it's important we get off on the right foot. Establish ground rules. Like punctuality. We should look for her."

"Really?" Nora asked. She suspected had it been herself missing, no one would have bothered.

"It'll only take a few minutes, especially if we split up. There aren't too many places Maggie could be, assuming she's on campus. Ashwin, would you mind checking the cafeteria? Alec, take a quick walk through the Wardroom and maybe the library? And, Nora, can you check the dorm? Maggie's room is in Alexandra Hall, like yours, only she's in the coed section."

"Figures," Nora muttered. "What will you do?"

"I'll stay here – she's probably on her way and it wouldn't do to have her come into an empty room. Do you mind, guys? It will only take ten minutes."

"And if we don't find Princess Maggie?" Nora snarked. "What then?"

"I don't know."

Daniel looked worried, Nora thought. He slung his thumbs into the belt loops of his jeans and looked out the window overlooking the Quad. Dozens of students loitered around, enjoying the last hour of sunshine. It was a beautiful evening and the setting sun cast large shadows over the courtyard. A sunbeam reflected off the adjacent dorm window, bathing Daniel in a golden light, making him look angelic. He was so ethereal it almost hurt to look at him and Nora turned away. The camaraderie they'd shared in the tunnel had vanished – she was back to feeling awkward.

When Daniel spoke again, his voice was soft. "It never occurred to me that Maggie wouldn't come. We need everyone for this to work. It's vital that we stick together, as a team."

"What's the big deal, man?" Alec wondered. "It's only our first day, chill a little. We've got the whole term to work on this."

Daniel hesitated. He seemed to weigh his words carefully and when he spoke, it was soft. "It's like this: I'm on an academic scholarship. I need to maintain a ninety-percent-average and this society assignment is worth ten-percent of our mark. I need to ace it if I'm to keep my GPA. I come from a large family and we can't afford tuition, let alone residence fees. If it doesn't work out, well..." The words trailed and he shrugged eloquently.

"Dude," Alec said awkwardly. "I didn't know. Sorry."

"No worries, mate," Ashwin said. "We'll find her."

Nora nodded, softening. "We'll take this seriously, Daniel. We won't goof off, right guys?"

"Right," Alec said. As he left the room, he muttered, "As serious as we can be hunting for ghosts."

**

In the Wardroom, Alec took a quick look at the bulletin board. There was a crowd of big guys around it so he guessed the team roster was posted early. He took a deep breath and jostled his way in. His stomach sank as he scanned the list twice, looking for his name. It wasn't on it.

But another name jumped out at him. Daniel O'Shea – DB. Same position he was going for. Son of a bitch.

**

Ashwin walked through the cafeteria looking for Maggie. Despite the late hour, the cafeteria was doing a booming business. Students had another ten minutes to get food before it closed for the evening, and judging from the trays piled high, this bunch was preparing for the apocalypse. They were allowed to take food back to the dorm rooms, but cooking appliances were forbidden. The scavenged food would be eaten cold, a prospect that didn't seem to faze the big oaf walking in front of him, his plate overflowing. The guy looked at him and Ashwin pointed. "The leaning tower of pizza?"

The guy stared at Ashwin quizzically. It was obvious he didn't get the joke. Ashwin nodded politely and let him pass.

Ashwin decided to check out the Quad – even though Daniel hadn't suggested it. It was such a glorious evening that everyone was naturally drawn to it. He walked quickly along the pathways, scanning the crowd, looking for Maggie's golden curls. For a moment he thought he'd spotted her sitting with a group of musicians, but, on closer inspection, realized it wasn't her.

Happy faces were everywhere. Melancholy stabbed through him and, not for the first time, Ashwin wished desperately he was back in Pondicherry with his family. He was painfully homesick and he doubted he would ever survive the year.

**

Daniel was looking out the window, arms crossed over his chest, when a giggling couple slunk into the room. They pressed against the far wall, making out.

"Excuse me," he said clearly. "This room is occupied."

They ignored him, as if he didn't exist. The boy lifted up the girl's shirt, exposing her breasts, not even attempting to hide them from Daniel's view.

Daniel turned away in disgust, staring into the courtyard. *Am I the only one who takes university seriously?* He wondered.

**

It was Nora who located Maggie. The other girl answered the door on the third knock. "Oh, hey, Nora."

Nora pushed the door open and stepped into the room. She shouldn't have. The dorm room was in chaos, boxes still unpacked and clothes strewn everywhere. Unlike Nora's room, this one was a single – same space but only one bed which left it

28

feeling surprisingly roomy after Nora's cramped quarters. It also cost a thousand dollars more per year – a waste of money, in Nora's view. "You forgot about our meeting."

Maggie looked at her blankly. She was wearing only a minuscule pair of pink panties and a ribbed tank. Her nipples were clearly visible though the thin fabric.

"The Spirit Seeker Society? You know, our first meeting? Tonight? Eight o'clock? Ringing any bells?"

"Oh, shit. I forgot." Maggie shrugged apologetically. She gestured at the rumpled bed and Nora became aware there was someone in it. The covers rustled slightly, falling open to reveal the naked chest of Kevin, the boy who'd offered to clear Maggie's lunch tray.

"Really?" Nora asked, her eyes narrowing. "You hooked up with a guy you just met a few hours ago?"

"Yeah. So?" Maggie began fumbling around, looking for her skirt and located a pair of shorts instead. She wiggled them on, hopping from one foot to the other. Nora noticed the blond didn't have a speck of cellulite anywhere. She thought of her own thighs and her lips thinned further.

"So, get ready to go. Everyone's waiting for you."

"Yeah... I think I'll pass," Maggie said. "I'm not really feeling it. What's the big deal, anyway?"

"The big deal, Miss Slutty Pants, is that it *is* a big deal. Other people are depending on you and I'm not letting you blow us off. Now, get your goddamn clothes on or I'll drag you down the hall the way you are, ass-cheeks exposed and perky little tits on display. Jesus."

Maggie stepped back. "Well, okay. Hold on a sec." She called over to the guy on the bed, "Hey... sorry, what's your name again?"

"Kevin." Nora and Kevin answered at the same time.

"Kev. I gotta split for a while. Hook up with you later in the Wardroom?"

"Sure, babe."

Nora rolled her eyes in disgust. "You've got two minutes to get ready. See you in the hall."

**

"Okay," Daniel said. "Let's begin now that we're all here."

The five members of The Spirit Seeker Society sat mutely around the table. Nora had been the first to arrive, practically dragging Maggie behind her. "Scram," Nora snarled at the lovebirds in the corner. "This room was booked."

Maggie looked lovely. Her face was flushed and her curls cascaded in tousled perfection. She wore no makeup, but her eyelashes were naturally dark and framed her blue eyes. Even her lips were bare of gloss, but they were puffy and sensuous – bedroom lips, Nora thought. Lips that had spent the afternoon kissing a strange boy whose name Maggie didn't even remember. She'd kept on her miniscule shorts, threw a loose cardigan over her tank top and a pair of flip-flops on her feet – taking less than thirty seconds to get ready, even though Nora had generously offered two minutes. Maggie looked stunning.

Ashwin arrived next, sitting quietly in the corner. He turned his face to the window, seemingly lost in thought. Alec followed moments later, pulling up a chair beside Ashwin, and his mood was dark and brooding. It was as if storm clouds were brewing internally. Daniel, too, was quiet, and everyone sat pensively around the table.

Nora decided to get the ball rolling. "If this group is to work effectively, we need to treat each other with respect, and that includes coming to meetings, on time." She looked pointedly at Maggie.

"Sorry," Maggie said. "It won't happen again." She smiled engagingly.

Nora noticed with irritation that everyone smiled back. Maggie was like that. She had a magnetic personality that made everyone want to forgive her. The Maggies in life had their path paved with jewels and flower petals. Everyone stumbled over themselves to make accommodations. Nora bet that no little boy called Maggie a witch. Ever.

"See that it doesn't. Or you're out of the group."

"That seems a little harsh," Ashwin said.

Daniel agreed. "The groups were assigned by the Dean. I doubt we can change them at will."

Nora bristled. Already she was painted as the bad guy when it should be Maggie. Group sentiment was turning against her. Except for Alec, who stared morosely out the window.

"Okay," Daniel said. "Does everyone have an idea of which spirit they'll try to seek?"

"I want to summon someone from the Halifax Explosion. I plan to concentrate on the Hydrostone area," Maggie said. She shifted slightly and her sweater fell open, exposing the thin ribbed tank and Nora could clearly see her nipple. Nora looked away. It made her feel uncomfortable... and something else. Something unidentifiable. She had an urge to place her hand on Maggie's breast, to stroke her nipple, to watch it spring to life. She shifted uncomfortably.

Ashwin cleared his throat. "I'd like to see if I can raise Major-General Robert Ross. He had a very interesting history: made a name for himself in the Napoleonic Wars, and then commanded the British troops in the War of 1812."

"What's the War of 1812?" Maggie wondered.

It was on the tip of Nora's tongue to make a scathing remark but she kept quiet. In truth, Nora wasn't that familiar with it either. They'd covered it in History 11, but that was seven years ago and she was sketchy on the details. Maggie's nipple winked invitingly and Nora's mouth went dry.

"In 1812, the Americans declared war on Britain. The Yanks were unhappy with a bunch of issues: trade restrictions, British support for the Natives, plus the Brits had the annoying habit of scooping American sailors and forcing them to serve on British ships which irritated the Yanks to no end. The Canadians sided with the Brits as they were incredibly peeved that the Yanks had burnt York, which is now known as Toronto, and were worried about further attacks. Were it not for the War of 1812, your entire country may well be flying under the stars and stripes. In retaliation, Robert Ross led the Canadians to burn down the White House, or at least attempt to. Ross is entombed in the Old Burying Ground, so I believe he is perfect for this assignment."

Alec looked over. "We burnt down the White House? How cool is that?"

"Immeasurably. Although I suppose the Yanks would disagree."

Daniel smiled. "Excellent, Ashwin. How about you Alec? Have you decided which spirit to seek?"

A frigid chill wafted abruptly through the air. No one commented on it. Nora developed goose bumps and Maggie's nipples became more prominent. And then it was gone, as quickly as it had come.

Alec rubbed his arms subconsciously and shot Daniel a moderately hostile glare. "I thought I'd check out *The Money Pit*, you know, on Oak Island? I did a project on it in high school and thought I could reuse my old notes. People have been trying to find that treasure for over two hundred years, and tons of people have died trying. Maybe the ghosts of Blackbeard and Captain Kidd can show me the money."

"What a grand idea," Ashwin said. "I don't believe I've ever heard of this Money Pit. And you, Nora?"

Nora tore her gaze away from Maggie's tank top and licked her lips. "Um, I thought I might see what I can find out at Pier 21. You said it yourself at our first meeting – as the entrance point for over a million immigrants, there's bound to be some spirit activity. If you believe in that sort of thing. Which I don't. It's stupid really, a colossal waste of time, but at the very least, I may learn some history which will be useful in other assignments."

"Good thinking," Maggie said. "There's an excellent museum there. Did you know that Pier 21 is considered Canada's Ellis Island?"

Nora's eyes widened in surprise. Maggie was surprisingly articulate. Perhaps there was a brain behind that slutty, perfect face.

"Plus," Maggie giggled, "Pier 21 is a *fantastic* area to shop, all sorts of organic goodies at the Seaport market. There was an awesome beer-fest there a few weeks ago – can't wait until next year when I'm old enough to legally go. It's exhausting sneaking in. But soooo worth it."

Nope, Nora amended. *Not so smart, just another spoiled daddy's girl.* "How about you, Daniel?" Nora asked, pointedly looking away from Maggie and the tank top that was now clearly showing the shadows of *two* nipples.

I hope to raise the spirit of Lila Rose," Daniel said. "She was a student here in 1969 and died under mysterious circumstances. She's been said to haunt these halls."

The lights flickered randomly and they all involuntarily sucked in their breaths, except for Daniel, who narrowed his eyes. "Maybe Lila's here right now," he remarked. "Trying to get our attention." He lowered his voice spookily. "Lila Rose, come out to play."

The lights flickered erratically and the chill returned, tenfold, as if an arctic breeze had blown in from the window. Even the heavy draperies were moving slightly – although the windows were closed. There was a strong feeling of being watched – of being spied on, and Nora noticed she wasn't the only one.   Then Daniel laughed, nervously, and the tension broke. The chill disappeared and the electricity steadied. "Huh. Maybe there is an argument for ghostly activity after all. It seems these old walls have stories to tell."

"Dude. That was creepy." Alec's eyes were wide and round. He didn't look quite so tough now.

"Yes," Daniel said, his handsome face looking... what? Troubled? Intrigued? Hopeful? "I say we call it a night. Let's meet once a week to report on progress, say Monday evenings at eight? I checked, and this room is available at that time. I tentatively booked it

– any conflicts? No? Great – first meeting of The Spirit Seeker Society is officially adjourned."

They shuffled out, all except for Alec. He looked at Daniel and said, "Congrats, man. You made the football team."

Daniel turned in surprise – he'd been staring at the curtains. "I did?"

"Yeah, dude, unless there's another Daniel O'Shea enrolled. The team list was just posted. I... I didn't make it."

"Oh, Alec, I'm sorry to hear that. I don't think they take many first year players."

"Yet you made it. DB – same position. I never saw you at tryouts. What high school did you go to? I thought they cut me because of my size, but you're not much bigger than me."

"No, I'm not." Daniel looked troubled. "Football team, eh? Imagine that. I never saw that coming." He left the room, leaving Alec alone. Alec noticed that Daniel hadn't answered any of his questions.

CHAPTER THREE

'They yearn for what they fear for' – Dante

Daniel O'Shea paced the second floor of the library. He knew as much about Lila Rose as he ever would. Her information was preserved in microfiche snippets of old newspaper clippings, but there wasn't that much to learn.

Lila Rose was found dead in her dorm room on October 31, 1969 – the cause of death was inconclusive. It was as if Lila Rose's heart simply stopped beating. There were faint marks around her throat, not vivid enough to leave real bruising, and oddly enough, the marks matched Lila's own hands. It was as if she'd gripped her own throat and stopped breathing.

That year, Halloween fell on a Friday, and by early evening the campus was in full party mode. The dorm bays were segregated and members of the opposite sex were forbidden to enter the other dorms. This did little to dissuade amorous suitors from trying, and on this night, with everyone in costume and alcohol flowing freely, staff gave up trying. Doors were propped open and it was a free for all.

Lila Rose was, by all accounts, a serious student. She occupied a shared room in Alexandra Hall with a small window overlooking the Quad. Lila had chosen not to participate in the Halloween revelry, instead focusing on her upcoming midterms. Her roommate, Chelsea Way, was a vivacious girl who loved to party and, more than once, Lila Rose had requested a roommate transfer on the grounds of incompatibility.

Her request was denied but Chelsea was routinely chastised, which contributed to a growing animosity.

Lila was, by all accounts, beautiful. Petite, dark curly hair cropped gamine-like; she had the effect of a young Audrey Hepburn. Even in the old black and white photos, her luminosity shone through. She had been valedictorian of her high school and entered King's with a near perfect GPA.

Lila did not have a boyfriend. She was friendly with her classmates, but distant. She had no known enemies. The secret of who killed Lila Rose died with her. Investigators never found a viable lead and the case remained open. It was if Lila Rose had been killed by a ghost.

1969 was a bad year for deaths at King's College. In addition to Lila, three students and two faculty members perished, a disproportionate number considering the student body numbered slightly over one thousand. One student died from accidental overdose, another committed suicide, and one died of pneumonia. Combined with the faculty members, it seemed the flag hanging from the Chapel spent much of 1969 at half-mast.

Lila Rose came from a middle-class family from Yarmouth, Nova Scotia. She was the oldest of four children and the first in her family to go to University. Her mother worked at a bank and her father was a milkman. Both Lila's parents passed away in their seventies, and her three siblings had scattered across the country. No one from the Rose family remained in Nova Scotia.

Daniel frowned at the information. It was all factual but gave little hint to who Lila Rose really was. What were her passions? What made her laugh or cry? What were her favorite foods? What kind of childhood illnesses had she sustained? He'd been hoping to find a clue to the essence of Lila Rose but the material was dry.

Maybe if he went to her old dorm room. He choose the underground tunnel that connected the residences, even though cutting across the Quad would have been the more direct route to Alexandra Hall.

Like the other day, the tunnel was uninhabited, and there was a creepiness that Daniel found mildly soothing. As he passed, a light bulb flickered erratically, and he paused, considering. Could this be an indication of ghostly activity? He would have to do further research to see if flickering electricity was a common poltergeist phenomenon.

He came to the room that was Lila Rose's. It was occupied by two first year students named Erin Hall and Jody Bentall. Campus residences were at capacity and there were no empty dorms, especially in a prime corner unit like this one. The door was locked but that was not a detriment to Daniel – he'd had years of practise at slipping through bolted doors. Once inside, he sat on one of the single beds and tried to conjure the image of Lila Rose. He knew the bunk on the right was hers, and when his mind remained blank, he tried the other bed. He envisioned her pretty face, the dark curls, tried to feel the essence of Lila Rose. But the room was barren. The ghost of Lila Rose did not seem interested in coming out to play.

**

Maggie ran into Nora in the cafeteria. "Oh, great," Maggie said, pulling out a chair without asking if Nora minded. "I've been looking all over for you. You are one hard lady to find."

Nora looked at Maggie's plate. "Lasagne?" she asked. "But you're vegan."

"It's meatless. Thankfully, the president agreed with my suggestion. There is going to be a vegan entree offered at every meal."

"You're kidding."

"Nope. He thought it was a great idea. I gathered two hundred signatures, so I think that helped."

"You're telling me he changed the cafeteria menu just because you asked? I can't believe it."

Maggie smiled. "Well, I went in prepared. Besides the petition, I brought literature to prove that a vegan diet is healthier, and I informed him that most universities already have a vegan alternative. Plus, I showed him how offering a meatless alternative is cost efficient and can actually save money in the long run."

"Huh. That was actually pretty smart of you."

Maggie tapped her forehead. "More than just a pretty face, you know."

Nora's eyes narrowed and Maggie laughed. "Oh, relax, it's just an expression. Look, I know we got off on the wrong foot. I want us to be friends. I'm going to the Hydrostone tomorrow after classes to look for my ghost and I was hoping you'd come with me."

"I don't think so."

"Oh, come on, it'll be a blast. There's a great second-hand clothing store, we can sort through the vintage bins. Halloween's not too far away and all the good stuff will be picked over if we wait until October. Plus, there is the most amazing bakery on Young Street. The pastry chef is from France and his croissants are to die for. I'll treat."

"Croissants aren't vegan."

"Shhh," Maggie laughed. "Don't tell anyone. I allow myself to cheat when it's worth it. Come on, Nora, please say you'll join me. It'll be more fun with you along and it'll give us a chance to get to know each other. We're the only two girls in the group – we need to stick together."

Nora thought of the peek-a-boo with Maggie's nipples and bit her lip. This was a bad idea. Nothing good could come from socializing with Maggie Bench. "Okay," she heard herself saying. It was as if her willpower curled up and died.

"Great. Meet me on the library steps at, say four o'clock? We can take the bus."

Nora was about to say something when two boys walked by, then stopped. "Hey, Maggie," one of them called. "You gonna be in the Wardroom tonight? There's a dart tournament."

"Sure thing, Jamie," Maggie called back. "Save me a seat."

Nora studied Maggie. "You collect boys like a flypaper traps insects."

"It's nothing," Maggie said. "I'm just friendly."

"Won't Kevin mind?"

"Who?"

"Kevin. You know, the guy from the other day, in your room. Isn't he your boyfriend?"

"God, no." Maggie shook her head. "He was just a hook up. Casual sex, nothing more. I might see him again, I might not. Who knows?"

Nora was silent. She couldn't speak if she wanted to. Is that what it was like to be a pretty girl? Guys all over you, no repercussions, university presidents changing menus on your whim? Plus, a body you were so comfortable with that you could strut around with tiny shorts and transparent tank tops? Jealousy threatened to choke her. She had a hard time breathing. It wasn't fair.

"It's set then?" Maggie asked, blithely unaware of Nora's inner turmoil. "Meet me tomorrow at four?"

Nora nodded, and Maggie flashed her one last grin, before bouncing off and linking her arms through the two guys. From the expressions on their faces, it seems Maggie Bench had just made their dreams come true.

**

Ashwin researched when the Old Burying Ground would be open for visitation. The stately wrought iron gates hung open, and aside from an elderly caretaker on the far side, the graveyard was empty. It was not a large space, two square city blocks, so it was hard to imagine that over twelve-thousand corpses were packed into it. These were old graves: the last internment was in 1844, over a century-and-a-half ago. Most of the graves remained unmarked. *The bodies,* Ashwin reflected, *must be literally stacked upon each other.* He tried to visualize twelve-thousand bodies lined shoulder-to-shoulder and figured, mathematically, the line would stretch for over eighty city blocks. For a moment, his mind lingered on what a spectacle that would be. Zombie-land.

Ashwin had a general idea of which direction to find Major-General Robert Ross's tomb. It took him twenty minutes, but he wasn't hurrying. There was something innately peaceful about graveyards. He thought of the cemeteries in Pondicherry, massive grounds which burst with color throughout the year. Here, green prevailed: grass and old trees, punctuated only by drab slabs of funeral grey.

Ross's tomb was taller than its neighbors, but not especially elaborate. The top was flat and inscripted – but the writing was faded and chipped from two centuries of harsh, north Atlantic weather. The epitaph was instructive, stating that Ross *'was killed at the commencement of an action which resulted in the defeat and flight of the troops of the United States near Baltimore, on the 12th Sept. 1814'*.

Ashwin leaned against the tomb and tried to visualize Robert Ross. He thought about the Major-General's many wartime victories which took him across continents and oceans. In the end he was to be felled by a couple of teenaged riflemen.

Ashwin did not believe in ghosts. He did not expect the body of Robert Ross to rise magically from his decaying tomb, but in the spirit of the assignment he gave it his best effort and settled in. It was amazingly serene here, especially after the noise and constant commotion of the university where it seemed nothing remained still. Certainly, the sounds of traffic filtered through the wrought iron fence but it was as if Ashwin was transported to another time.

What would it have been like to live two hundred years ago? To be a career soldier, to have your life mapped out for you as you bounced from battleground to battleground, growing steadily in both reputation and skill?

His preliminary research indicated that Ross was a hands-on leader. He personally led his troops, riding forth upon magnificent stallions, resplendent in his regimental dress. From all accounts, Ross's luck ran out in 1814. First, he was shot in the neck, but that didn't deter him. Later that year, attacking Washington, he would narrowly miss death, having his horse shot out from under him. Then: three strikes, you're out. A few weeks later, Ross would take a fatal bullet.

So much passion, such drama, dying for one's country.

Ashwin shook his head. Some men were born to create history, and others, such as himself, were afflicted with an overpowering homesickness. Ashwin Pawar hung his head in shame. He thought of his father. What would Papa think of this assignment? Would Papa consider searching for ghosts in ancient graveyards an honorable endeavor or a frivolous exercise?

"I am trying, Papa," Ashwin whispered. "I am trying to assimilate, to make friends. I am trying to bring honor to the Pawar name by succeeding in all areas, no matter how trivial." Ashwin wiped his reddened eyes and runny nose on the back of his hand, sniffling.

He would come back tomorrow when he was in a better frame of mind.

**

Maggie and Nora stepped off the bus and onto Young Street, and into the chic yet quaint shopping area. The Hydrostone was one of the more notorious neighborhoods in Halifax. In 1917, a French munitions ship called the *Mont-Blanc* was fully loaded with explosives, en route to Bordeaux. It was navigating the busy harbor when it collided with the Norwegian ship *SS Imo*. A fire broke out and people flocked to the waterfront to watch the *Mont-Blanc* burn. It took twenty minutes for the ship to blow – and what happened next rewrote Halifax's history.

The resulting explosion was so catastrophic that the world hadn't seen anything like it, and wouldn't again until the Atomic Bomb made an appearance decades later. Every window shattered on both sides of the harbor, trees snapped like twigs, and iron rails melted and bent. Buildings were flattened and fragments of the *Mont-Blanc* rained for five kilometres – twisted hunks of red-hot metal that impaled anything or anyone unfortunate enough to be in its way. A massive two-square-kilometre radius was obliterated and the damage extended to every part of the city. Nothing and no one remained unscathed. Fifteen hundred people died instantly, another five hundred would succumb to injuries, and another nine thousand were wounded. The noise and vibrations from the explosion were felt three hundred kilometres away.

Then came the tsunami. A wall of water eighteen metres high, generated by the force of the explosion flooded the streets, drowning those few people who had somehow managed to survive.

On the graveyard of that devastation sprang the Hydrostone – an area of ten-square-city-blocks modeled after an English-style garden suburb, with wide boulevards and tree-lined streets. The row-style housing was built of concrete cinder blocks, or hydro-stones, from whence it got its name. Almost a century later, the Hydrostone existed as a trendy neighborhood filled with hipsters and artists and upwardly mobile young families.

"Let's eat first," Maggie suggested, opening the door to Julien's. Maggie waved to people in the corner and called the server by name. "The usual, Andrea," she said. "Make it two. I'll order for my friend."

Nora bristled at the idea of Maggie ordering without consulting her but held her tongue. It felt surprisingly good to be connected to Maggie, like she'd received entrée to the in-crowd. They settled into a small table near the front window and when Nora bit into her chocolate croissant, she was lifted to a whole new level. "Oh, sweet Jesus," she said, her mouth full. "This is the best thing I've tasted. Ever."

"Told you," Maggie said.

"I wonder if they sell them by the dozen? I want a *crate* of these."

"Don't bother. They never taste the same at home. I don't know what it is."

"Even if they were half as good at home, they'd still be amazing," Nora said, licking the last few crumbs from her lips. She really wanted another croissant, maybe an almond one this time, but forced herself to remain seated. She would not make a pig of herself in front of her dining companion. "How are we supposed to find a ghost without looking like lunatics?"

"I was thinking about that," Maggie said. "There's a fortune-teller down the street. She reads Tarot cards, crystal balls, palms, that kind of thing; she has a reputation for being a good medium. It might be a place to start."

"Or a place to get ripped off," Nora snorted.

"Gotta keep an open mind," Maggie said. "What do we have to lose?"

"Twenty bucks?"

"More like fifty. But it'll be fun and as it's my ghost hunt, I'll pay."

"What are you, a trust-fund baby?"

"Mmm, I guess you could say that." She tossed a ten dollar bill on the table and stood.

"Really?" Nora gaped. "You're leaving a ten buck tip? For coffee and croissants? Geez, she didn't even serve us – we had to carry our own food."

Maggie shrugged. "Hey, it's good karma. The universe pays back tenfold. Try it sometime – you'd be surprised."

There was a thirty minute wait at *Madam Denicci's Psychic Emporium*, so they elected to visit the vintage shop to kill time. Nora caught their reflection in the storefront window and it brought her back to reality: her hulking form towering over Maggie in an ominous, cartoonish way. Her shoulders slumped in defeat – no matter how much things changed, they always stayed the same. She followed Maggie into the thrift store. "Hey, Celeste," Maggie called to the shopkeeper. "Did you save me any good stuff?"

"Geez, do you know everyone in this city?" Nora grumbled. Even though she had grown up in a much smaller town, she couldn't think of a single business where they knew her by name. "Hey," Nora added, sounding surprised. "This place is actually pretty decent."

"I know, right? Once a month they have '*Stuff a Bag Day*' – anything you can fit in for ten bucks. I always try to come the next day when the new stock comes in. That's when you find the nicest stuff, before it gets picked over. One time I found a beaded handbag with the original price tag still attached – six hundred dollars. I got it for three bucks. There's also a story about someone who found jewels sewn into the lining of a fur coat. You never know where people will try to hide stuff and it just floats around waiting to be found."

"Wait – I don't get it. You're rich, but you dumpster-dive in second hand stores?"

Maggie laughed. "It's fun. It's the *hunt* that counts, like being a treasure seeker. Sure, I could go to the mall and drop a few hundred on designer jeans, but it's a rush to find a pair of True Religions for five dollars. Hey, what size are you? I'll keep an eye open when searching through the bins."

Size fourteen. On a good *day.* Nora wasn't planning to say it out loud. "Um, no thanks, I'm okay for clothes – I'll check out the used books. Looks like an eclectic selection. Only a buck a book? Maybe I'll find some textbooks in here – they cost a fortune."

Ten minutes later, Maggie ambushed Nora with a basket of clothes. "Hey, come to the dressing room, will you? I want to try this stuff on – need your opinion."

Nora followed doggedly behind, sitting in the corner of the small, squalid dressing room. A thin curtain hung to block the dressing room from view, and it didn't quite stretch all the way to the edges. Every time someone walked by it wafted open but Maggie seemed oblivious. She stripped off her clothes in moments, standing in the tiniest black lace panties Nora had ever seen – what did they call it? Butt-floss? It was apparent from the lack of fabric that Maggie was a fan of waxing – not a stray hair in sight. Maggie had a pierced navel and the tiniest of tattoos above her left hip – a Celtic symbol of some sort. Also, no bra, and Maggie's tanned breasts – small but perfectly formed, stood at eye level with Nora. Nora's mouth went dry and she tried not to stare. Tried to look somewhere else. Anywhere.

"What do you think?" Maggie asked, pirouetting in the small space, showing off a sparkly tee-shirt.

I don't know what to think, Nora thought. *I'm so confused.* Maggie's body was taut and smooth; Nora felt like running her hands all over, had the urge to suckle Maggie's rosebud nipples, itched to probe her fingers under the butt-floss and finding out how little hair there really was. What would Maggie taste like? "Um, I gotta get out of here, feeling claustrophobic." Nora stammered, fleeing the room.

Oh fuck, Nora thought, catching her breath. *I think I might be gay.*

CHAPTER FOUR

'The decent into Hell is easy' – Virgil

Madam Denicci scowled at them. She narrowed her eyes, looked from one girl to the other and watched them speculatively. It made Nora feel remarkably uncomfortable and she noticed even Maggie shifted slightly.

"You are in grave danger," Madam Denicci proclaimed after an interminable amount of time. She hadn't done anything yet – hadn't cracked open the Tarot cards, nor peered into her crystal ball. Hadn't even taken a peek at their palms, just stared at them like she was the predator and they were prey. Nora frowned. She'd read enough mystery novels to know this wasn't how it was supposed to go.

"We came to ask about finding a ghost," Maggie began.

"You are surrounded by spirits," Madam Denicci said eerily, waving her hand in a theatrical flourish.

"Really?" Maggie squealed. "That's perfect. We're doing an assignment, for school. I need to contact someone from the Halifax Explosion, and I'd prefer a female, if possible."

Madam's eyes narrowed further, making her appear serpentine. "Uh," Nora said, "I don't think it works that way. It's not *Ghost's-R-Us*, where you can select your style and size."

Madam's eyes slid from Maggie and studied Nora. The woman didn't speak, and her gaze held Nora's for an uncomfortably long time, the moments stretching until Nora felt she must tear herself away. It was as if the woman was seeing into her soul.

In a deft movement that caught them by surprise, the woman's hand lashed out suddenly and grasped Nora's. "Ah, just as I thought," she murmured, studying the palm. She clucked her tongue in disproval.

"Now you," she said to Maggie.

Maggie leaned forward. "Alrighty, make it fabulous. No negative readings for me, please."

The fortune teller ignored her, gripping Maggie's hand tightly, peering intently. She harrumphed suddenly and released her, and Maggie backed her chair up a few inches. Maggie had stopped smiling – she actually looked worried, Nora thought. Just the tiniest bit and her brow wrinkled charmingly. When Maggie frowned, her dimples disappeared entirely.

Madam Denicci shuffled the Tarot cards and began to deal them into a cross-like pattern. "This is the Celtic Cross Spread," she said, speaking quickly, her voice gravelly in the small room. Her fingers danced. "It will clarify what surrounds you."

As the final card was laid, Maggie's eyes flew to the fortune-teller.

Nora looked at Maggie and at the card. She couldn't see what the fuss was about. Sure, it looked ominous: a dark tower, aflame, with bodies falling.

"This is what surrounds you now," Madam Denicci began. "You have the power to change your fate, to alter your paths, but you must work together. Where one falters both will fail."

"Tell us how to change it," Maggie said. Her eyes were round, and Nora's arms prickled with goose-bumps, even though the room was warm and stuffy.

The medium ignored them, her words tumbling forth like a cornucopia of doom. "Here." She stabbed at the center card, her voice had grown deeper. *It was for effect*, Nora told herself. *She was trying to scare them.* "Ah, the Seven of Swords. Something will be stolen from you. You must guard your treasures. The Devil crosses you– you are trapped of your own violation. What falls beneath you is the Eight of Cups. You will notice it is upside down? This reversal signifies your inability to move on. You will be stuck here."

Nora rubbed her arms unconsciously, trying to warm her chilled skin. Why was she so cold? Her eyes were drawn involuntarily to the fortune-teller's fingers which hovered over another card, this one depicting a naked man and woman. "The Lovers," the medium said, her voice accusatory. *She knows,* Nora thought guilty. *She knows I'm attracted to Maggie.* "This is your recent past, and it represents choices – good and bad, which brought you to this point. You are victims, true, but your decisions led you here, will continue to lead you. You must select wisely."

"This isn't making sense –" Nora began, and Madam cut her off with a warning glare.

"The Hanged Man crowns you. There is a period of waiting and you must use this time wisely. Do not view the world through unseeing eyes. See how he hangs upside down? You must look from different angles, from a new perspective if you are to see clearly."

Maggie glanced at Nora with a quick intake of breath. She became very still.

"Before you lies the Three of Swords. This is your immediate future, you understand. This card signifies heartbreak. Literally, it can be mean heart pain or surgery, a cutting of the flesh. Beware of injury, beware of pain."

Nora looked at the card closely: a large red heart stabbed through with three swords. She had to admit, it didn't look promising. She looked back at the fortune-teller, her mouth dry, at a loss for words. Her immediate future should involve her fleeing from this nasty little room but her feet were leaden: as if glued to the floor.

"As with the Devil, your restriction is self-imposed," Madam Denicci continued relentlessly. "Again, you have the choice to extricate yourself from your future, but you hesitate." She didn't name the card, and Nora looked at it. Again, ominous: a white-robed woman, bound and blindfolded, surrounded by a ring of giant swords. The roiling storm clouds blew the woman's dark hair with a ferocity that transcended the card.

"She looks like you," Maggie whispered.

It was true. Although the illustrated girl was prettier, with finer features. Yet the essence was there, as if Nora was looking at a caricature of herself. "And the girl on the Lovers card looks like you," Nora answered. The face was Maggie's, although not the coloring. It was uncanny.

"Five of Swords," Madam Denicci was saying, "shows you are surrounded by a negative energy. A one-upmanship. You are pawns in his game, and he does not play fairly."

"Can't play the game if you don't know the rules," Maggie murmured and the medium nodded sagely.

"The Moon," Madam Denicci continued, "shows more will be revealed. You do not have all the facts. There is deception; dark powers at work. Attend to your dreams – night magic may show you paths unclear during the day."

"And the Tower," Maggie said, pointing to the final card. "Catastrophic change."

"The breaking apart of all structures."

Nora looked at the card closely. Almost medieval feeling, with the tall black tower rising from the raging sea. It reminded her of the university with its formal, stone facade.

"But what can it all mean?" Maggie asked, ashen.

Madam remained silent then drew one last card. "For clarification," she explained. "Ah." Madam Denicci's eyes swung through the small, airless room, considering. "Your decisions are myriad – your path will remain unclear until you choose."

"That didn't help," Nora sputtered. "It's only made it worse. More confusing. What decisions? What choices are you talking about? Look, you're just trying to scare us into giving you more money – and it's not working. Come on, Maggie, let's get out of here. This woman's a fraud."

Maggie shrugged her off. "The ghost," Maggie asked, her voice holding a tinge of desperation. "Will she help or harm?"

"It is undetermined," Madam Denicci stated, frowning.

Nora gaped. It was as if they were speaking their own private language.

"What ghost?" Nora asked. *Why were her legs so leaden? Why couldn't she move?*

"There are more forces to deal with. Again, things are not as they seem."

Not as they seem? What kind of copout was that? Bland, generic advice – completely unhelpful. That is, if one considered a fortune-teller a viable source of information. Which Nora didn't. "What ghost?" She repeated, getting cross. She moved her foot a little. It was as if she was wearing cement shoes. "What ghost are you two lunatics talking about?"

"Why, the one beside you," Madam Denicci stated.

"Can't you see her, Nora?" Maggie asked.

Nora raised her eyes, her mouth opening to tell them to knock it off, to quit trying to scare her. What kind of idiot did they think she was? This was someone's idea of a sick joke and it wasn't very funny.

But her mouth snapped shut. Hovering beside her was the image of a woman. Shimmering, wavering, her feet a few inches off the ground. Her image was solid yet transparent – as if she was only fifty-percent completed. The woman moved and the image wavered, fading for an instant, before being become clear again, as if it had just received an infusion of energy.

"Holy shit," Nora said, and she slunk back in her chair. Her eyes rolled up under her skull and for the first time in her life, Nora Berkowitz fainted.

CHAPTER FIVE

'You have known,
O'Gilgamesh,
What interests me,
To drink from the Well of Immortality.
Which means to make the dead
Rise from their graves...'
– Anonymous, The Epic of Gilgamesh

Alec watched the football practise, from a distance. He could not bring himself to join the crowd of students sitting idly on the cement bleachers overlooking Wickwire Field. He'd walked across campus from King's, wearing a hoodie despite the warmth of the late afternoon sun so as not to be recognizable. It was a poor choice, he was sweltering. He stopped in at the student union building on the Dalhousie campus to purchase a frozen yogurt, then made himself semi-invisible behind a large oak tree across the parking lot from the field. It wasn't the best vantage point, but he could see enough.

He should be on this team. Yes, he was on the small side, but he was fast. The coach had been sympathetic. "Son, we had a large tryout this year. The football team is a new addition for Dal, and it's become more popular than we'd hoped for. Last year, we were crying for defensive backs. But this year, we have almost all the veteran players returning. Bulk up a little, add some muscle, and come see me next year."

Alec hadn't considered not making the team. This wasn't even a CIS team, so he'd been realistic in his expectations. Or so he thought. It was the reason he allowed his parents to enrol him at King's. His parents had been working toward this goal since he was in grade school, and they steadfastly refused to consider other options. His mother wrote his entrance essays; his father vetted his high school activities, so on paper, he was well-rounded. His resume was rife with volunteer stats, athletic achievements, and carefully selected student clubs. But Alec himself had very little involvement – even his high school newspaper bylines were a farce – his parents had penned the stories. And now, without his parents monitoring his every move and controlling his academic input, the work load was too rigorous. The professors advised four hours of homework for every hour of class. Yeah, right. That wasn't going to happen.

As it was, he barely understood anything the professors said. The words they used: it was like they weren't speaking English. And the volume of reading – Alec groaned thinking about it. They started right out the gate with *The Epic of Gilgamesh* and Virgil's *The Aeneid.* Talk about confusing. Even when the professor explained passages, Alec still didn't have the faintest clue what was going on.

Someone threw an incomplete pass on the gridiron and the coaches started hollering. Simple words, lots of swearing. Alec sighed. *That* was the language he understood.

At least the food was decent – he could have pizza for every meal. And the Wardroom was awesome. He'd played darts there last night, made a few friends. As an underage student, he wasn't allowed to order beer, but when no one was looking, he helped himself to the half-drunk glasses on the table. He was a November baby so he hadn't even turned eighteen yet. Which meant a full year plus two months before he was legally allowed to drink. It sucked.

Another pass thrown on the field, this one completed. The players and the crowd went wild: it was if they'd won the Super Bowl. Everyone was clapping the receiver on the back; the quarterback was dancing a little jig. *For crying out loud,* Alec thought, *it's only a practise.* He stood abruptly. He couldn't watch anymore.

He tossed his frozen yogurt into the garbage and slowly retraced his steps back to King's.

**

Ashwin was in a better frame of mind. He'd made a list of all the things he disliked about Pondicherry and mentally recited them until he felt less homesick. India's oppressive heat – it would be cooler than summer but the average temperature in September was still a hundred degrees. And the monsoon season was just starting – he would not miss that. Even though he'd spent his entire life in Pondicherry, Ashwin still found the monsoon season left him feeling like a wet dishrag.

Plus the noise – it never ended. Constant blaring of taxi horns, street vendors hawking their wares at every corner, always the need to barter for everything. How pleasant it was to simply pay a fair price without haggling.

The university itself was a dream. People were respectful, the academia was exquisite and this first week of lectures proved sublime. It was interesting without being overly challenging. Some of the texts he'd previously read, and when he heard other students groaning about the difficulty of the material, he cocked his head in surprise. It was simply a matter of listening to the professors and carefully following instructions. Always an avid reader, Ashwin enjoyed the solitude of his tiny single dorm room and found the hours evaporated as he was lost in prose.

His cursed insomnia had become an ally. During the long, dark hours he fought sleep, Ashwin allowed his mind to drift through the day's lectures, examining all angles and possibilities while the clock ticked mercilessly toward morning. The fatigue would eventually catch up to him, he knew, but for now, his mind was alive with the abundance of information flowing his way.

The epic poem of *Gilgamesh* was the perfect example: a fascinating insight into one of mankind's earliest written works. One could call it the original buddy-novel – and this was the angle that Ashwin planned to expostulate upon in his thesis. They were only supposed to read the first twenty pages, yet Ashwin was so transfixed he couldn't put it down, reading into the wee hours in one sitting.

And he planned to read it again. Today, in the graveyard, beside the remains of Robert Ross. It seemed especially fitting to champion the fictional Gilgamesh's pursuit for immortality against the tomb of a mortal whose own quest was not so very different.

**

Rush hour had long ebbed by the time Nora and Maggie caught the bus home, yet the bus was still busy. They were lucky to score a seat together. Maggie suggested taking a taxi but Nora refused. She was already embarrassed enough about fainting. She didn't want to cause further fuss, and unlike Maggie, her money was carefully allotted and Nora couldn't afford her half of the cab fare. Even though Maggie had offered to pay, Nora did not wish to be further in debt to Maggie Bench.

"That was... *intense*," Maggie said.

"I don't want to talk about it."

"Are you sure you don't need to see a doctor? You hit your head pretty hard."

"When you're as tall as I am, you have a long way to fall," Nora said ruefully. Truth was, she still had a sizable goose egg on the back of her skull.

"You're lucky to be so tall," Maggie said, and Nora was surprised to hear the wistful tone of her voice.

"Are you kidding me? I'm a circus freak."

Maggie laughed. "Get real. Try being so short that all you see is the back of everyone's shirt. I'm lucky the auditorium has stadium seating, otherwise I'd never be able to see the professor."

"Huh. I hadn't thought about that."

Maggie slipped her hand into Nora's and squeezed. "What about the... ghost? That was freaky."

The old lady sitting in the seat ahead turned around and gawked at them. "Mind your own business, you old bat," Nora said pointedly, and the woman turned around in a huff. "It was... yeah." *Freaky. Insane. Crazy. Take your pick: any adjective would fit.*

Nora still couldn't get her head wrapped around it. After she'd come to, the ghost was gone. "It must have been a trick of some kind. *No way* was that real."

Maggie bit her lip. "Let's talk about it back at school, okay? Come to my room?"

Nora thought about the untidy mess, clothing flung everywhere, the rumpled bed. The lacy undergarments. Her mouth went dry. "Uh, come to my room instead."

"Okay," Maggie said, squeezing Nora's hand tighter. "But be warned: I might be sleeping over. I'm wayyyy too freaked to sleep alone after that."

**

The Old Burying Ground was again empty, save for the same, elderly caretaker. He ignored Ashwin, leaving Ashwin to wander among the tombstones undisturbed. Many were indistinct – some of the epitaphs were completely illegible, although others were remarkably clear and embellishments such as angel wings, cherubim and trumpets were popular. Most were simple: bearing a name and lifespan. Some held terms of endearment: *beloved husband, faithful wife, cherished child.* Those were the hardest, to see the graves of children and infants. He halted in front of one in particular, his eyes widening slightly as he realized it held the corpses of six children. An entire family? Perhaps, he thought. What kind of tragedy could have befallen them? Likely they died of illness, cholera perhaps, or influenza. The inscription was poignant:

> *What once had virtue, grace and wit*
> *Lies mouldering now beneath our feet*
> *Poor mansions for such lovely guests*
> *Yet here they sweetly take their rest.*
> *Cold is their bed and dark their rooms*
> *Yet angels watch around their tombs*
> *Pleased they patrol, nor sleep, nor faint*
> *They only watch their fellow saints*
> *Till the loud mansions of the skies*
> *Relieve their guards and bids them rise.*

The sentiment renewed Ashwin's longing for his own siblings and he moved on, quickening his pace, then pausing as another gravestone caught his eye. Ashwin felt his mouth quirk before he stilled it. Surely his amusement was disrespectful as he read about poor James Bossom, who apparently was *"Willfully Murdered On the Morning of the 8th of August 1839 by Smith D. Clark in the 23rd year of his Age."* Apparently slander laws in 1839 were not what they were today. Perhaps James Bossom would be an interesting spirit to resurrect. Ashwin was curious if Smith D. Clark was indeed his killer, or simply deigned to be maligned in perpetuity.

Ashwin took a shortcut across the graveyard, taking care not to step on the tombs. The thought chilled him, despite the warmth of the late summer evening, as if a frigid pocket of air surrounded him. He glanced up and located the caretaker. No matter where Ashwin was in the graveyard, it seemed the old-timer was at the furthest point. Ashwin frowned. He would like to talk to the old duffer, mine him for nuggets. The old fellow probably had some very interesting stories to tell and might even be able to enlighten Ashwin about the appearance of ghosts in the Old Burying Ground. Or impart more information about Major-General Ross.

Ashwin settled beside Ross's grave, as he had the other day, and let his mind wander.

**

Maggie and Nora fell into Nora's room, gasping for breath. Despite the bump on her head, which hurt like hell, Nora felt euphoric, giddy. Had they really seen a ghost?

As usual, Nora's roommate was absent. Nora barely saw the girl. Like herself, Ann was mousy, studious and socially ill at ease. On paper, they were the perfect match. In reality, they had nothing to say to each other, and Ann seemed uncomfortable in Nora's towering presence. Ann had fashioned a privacy curtain around her bunk, and spent little time in the room, appearing only late at night to sleep. When she was there, she would nod to Nora formally, and slip inside the curtain. Nora could not have been more pleased. As an only child, she was not used to sharing space, especially one as minuscule as this. Also, like Nora, Ann's belongings were few – and despite that fact that two women occupied a space of no more than eight by ten feet, it didn't seem claustrophobic.

Maggie flung aside Ann's curtain and flounced on the bed. She had total disregard for the other's private space, throwing her body out lengthwise and stretching. Yesterday, this action would have annoyed Nora. Today she found it charming. Oh, to be as carefree and present as Maggie Bench.

"How did you not see that ghost, Nora?" Maggie squealed, hugging Ann's pillow to her chest. "I mean, she was there almost from the instant we arrived."

"Was she really?" Nora asked. "I didn't notice her."

"She appeared during the Tarot reading. Indistinct at first, and then, all of a sudden, she was there. Freaky, yes, but she seemed harmless. I didn't get the feeling she was a malevolent spirit."

"No? I couldn't say. The moment I saw her, I well..." Nora mimicked crashing backwards and both girls dissolved into a fit of laughter.

"This isn't funny," Nora said, finally. "We shouldn't be laughing at this. It seems disrespectful."

"No, you're right. But I shouldn't think she'd mind. She looked like a friendly ghost." Maggie hummed a few bars of *Casper, The Friendly Ghost's* theme song, and that did it – the giggles started again. "Seriously, though. We're going to have to go back. I wonder if the Spirit will see us somewhere else? Madam Denicci was scarier than the ghost."

Nora sobered. "She was, wasn't she? What was all that nonsense about how we're doomed, making wrong choices, someone is deceiving us, blah blah blah."

"Yeah, that was creepy, too. And to finish with the Tower card. That is *never* good." Maggie shivered suddenly. "Geez, it's freezing in here." She began sifting through Ann's stuff, grabbed a sweater and put it on. "You were smart to ask for a double room, Nora. I'm wayyyy too freaked to sleep alone tonight. Can I stay here?"

"There's no space for a third body – this room is no bigger than a pigeon hole."

"Maybe your roomie could switch with me tonight? Do you think, Nora? Or you could sleep in my room. Please?"

Suddenly, Nora wanted nothing more than to have Maggie Bench as her roommate. "I can ask her," Nora said slowly. "She probably wouldn't mind."

Maggie bounded off the bed and catapulted onto Nora's, throwing her arms around Nora's neck. "You are the best, Nora. The best."

CHAPTER SIX

'There is in every one of us, even those who seem to be most moderate, a type of desire that is terrible, wild, and lawless' – Plato

The second official meeting of the Spirit Seeker Society was remarkably different from the first. By now, everyone had settled into campus life, and in the adaptable way of humans, they greeted each other like old friends.

The football team had played their first home game against the St. John Sea Wolves, and won by a field goal. Alec did not attend, and secretly wished for the team to lose. He knew it was sour grapes, but he couldn't help himself. He and Ashwin had shown up for the first ball hockey intramural and found, much to their surprise and delight, that it was a very silly affair indeed. A few of the teams seemed to take it seriously, but most came in costume: dressed up as transvestites, or chickens, or in the case of two separate teams, painted blue and sporting horns: The Blue Devil motif was King's mascot. An argument ensued about which Blue Devil's team should keep their outfits, with compelling arguments on both sides, until it was decided that they'd play a game of ball hockey and the winner would take all. The losers removed their horns and became known as the Holy Smurfs.

Ashwin had returned to the Old Burying Ground each afternoon after classes and sat against the Major-General's tomb. He found himself talking to Ross as if he was a confidant, and extolled the virtues of Pondicherry, confessing his shameful secret of homesickness. If the spirit of Ross was interested, he did not let it show, and did not deign to make an appearance. Ashwin did not believe he really would, but kept up his cathartic monologue all the same. Sometimes the graveyard had other visitors, but most times Ashwin would find himself alone, aside from the caretaker who always stayed on the far edge of the graveyard. Once or twice, Ashwin was compelled to raise his hand in greeting, but it was never returned, nor was Ashwin acknowledged.

Nora phoned her mother, dutifully, on Friday. That was the agreement. At age twenty-four, Nora certainly didn't need to check in with her parents, but she'd promised to keep in touch. Nora was probably the only student who didn't have a cell phone, and she used the landline in her room. The Berkowitzes were delighted to hear their daughter was faring well.

She didn't tell them about Maggie or the Spirit Seeker Society, but said she'd made friends, and that was all the Berkowitzes, an older couple who'd only had the one change-of-life baby, could ask for.

After a whirlwind of activity, entirely orchestrated by Maggie, Nora and Maggie became roommates. First, Maggie offered an exchange to Nora's roommate Ann – who jumped at the bait to switch her double for a single, especially when Maggie said it was already paid for and wouldn't cost the other student a dime. Ann could have the private room for the same price as the double. Then, with an expediency that amazed Nora, Maggie switched their room for a nicer unit on the third floor in a corner unit. Not only was it considerably larger than the previous room, which had faced the parking lot, but this new room had a south facing view of the Quad, and they'd get sun for most of the day. The difference in atmosphere was astounding.

"How did you get them to agree?" Nora asked.

"It was easy. Something happened to freak them out – they were scared to stay. They heard voices and other weird noises."

Nora laughed. "Tell the truth: it was you, wasn't it? Calling spooky things under their door."

"No, but brilliant idea, wish I'd thought of it. Probably just the wind howling. You know how these old buildings are. Now, which bed do you want?"

"This one," Nora said, sitting with a thump. "Now remember your promise: keep your side tidy. I can't live in a pigsty."

"Sure," Maggie said, tossing her clothing basket high in the air so the room rained clothing. "How is that?"

Nora laughed, dislodging a pair of lime green panties from her pillow. "Perfect. But this doesn't really go with my color scheme so you can take it back."

In the end, Maggie managed to keep her area tidy for three hours, and when the mess threatened to overflow onto Nora's side, Nora straightened it up. Oddly, she didn't mind. Folding Maggie's dainty, sexy clothing was actually kind of fun.

**

"That is awesome," Alec said, when the girls told the group about their ghostly encounter. "When are you going back?"

Nora and Maggie exchanged a glance. "We went again on Saturday, but nothing happened. We strolled up and down the Hydrostone until our legs just about fell off," Maggie explained.

"And nothing?"

"Nothing," Nora admitted. "If Maggie hadn't seen it too, I would have thought I imagined the whole thing." Truthfully, Nora still didn't believe it a hundred percent. She'd only seen the ghost for the barest of instances before she'd conked out.

The girls had discussed Madam Denicci's forecast in great detail, pondering over every snippet. "As long as we make good choices," Maggie theorized, "we should be fine."

"But don't tell the boys," Nora said. "They will make fun of us."

Maggie agreed. She was planning on returning later in the week, without telling Nora. Nora was great, but in truth, they'd been spending every moment together and Maggie was finding it claustrophobic.

"What about you, Nora? Have you made any progress at Pier 21?" Daniel wondered.

Nora frowned. "Not really. I've done some research and need to go the museum. The problem is, it's always so crowded there – even if there was a ghost, it wouldn't show itself."

"Don't be so sure," Daniel said. "Some ghosts love crowds. They can be pranksters, you know. If someone had a good sense of humor while alive, that tendency would remain."

"You sound like a ghost expert," Alec said. "Surprised you even have time for it considering all the football practises."

Daniel let the jibe slide. "Let's just say, the spirit world is a hobby, of sorts. How about you, Ash?"

Ashwin looked at the floor. "Respectable progress." He did not elaborate.

"And you, Alec?"

Alec bristled. He hadn't even begun this dumb assignment. Between classes, homework, daily gym workouts, intramurals and decompressing in the Wardroom, he had no spare time. He'd been trying to complete a paper about Gilgamesh but hadn't gotten further than his thesis statement. "I've been doing research," he fabricated, "but I really need to go there. Hey, how about next Saturday? Anyone up for a road trip? I can borrow a car, and we can check out Oak Island. If the weather's good, we could stop at Queensland Beach – tons of hot babes there. Whaddya guys say? Grab a bucket of chicken, take a break from academia?"

Maggie jumped up and high-fived Alec. "I'm totally in," Maggie said, enthusiastically. "I'll bring a Frisbee and a salad."

Ashwin perked up. He'd been dreading the weekend with no classes. This past one dragged relentlessly. "Yes, that sounds enjoyable. We can make a full day of it. I'll bring samosas, perhaps a curried vegetable dish for you, Maggie."

"Can you bring beer?" Alec asked hopefully.

"I told you, I don't drink."

"C'mon Ash, you're the only one old enough to buy it."

"I'll bring beer," Nora said, surprising everyone. "But I'm not putting on a bathing suit. No way."

Alec slapped her hand in salute and Nora flushed. She'd never been high-fived before and she wasn't quite sure what to do with her hand afterwards, so she folded it primly in her lap.

"What about you, Daniel?" Maggie asked. She turned the full wattage of her smile on him and he frowned.

"Uh, can't. The football team is away next weekend – game in Prince Edward Island." Daniel ran his fingers through his tousled light brown hair. He legitimately looked upset. The group tried to come up with an alternate date but nothing fit. "Don't worry about it," Daniel said. "Go, have fun, and tell me all about it at the next meeting."

Nora eyed him. She wanted to get him alone, just to talk, but couldn't think of a way to approach him without looking like an idiot. Aside from the first day, when he'd walked her to her dorm room, she hadn't seen him. She kept looking around the auditorium for him but couldn't spot him. Although, with two hundred students in the FYP lectures plus over a thousand students on campus, it was impossible to see everyone. She'd run into Alec and Ashwin on occasion and they always smiled in greeting. It was remarkable, Nora thought. An instant group of friends, and what a difference that made. Perhaps the professors knew what they were doing when they issued this assignment.

The disappointment she felt upon learning that Daniel wouldn't be joining them was rife. The hunger for his company was insidious, and she chastised herself. No way did a girl who looked like her have any business mooning over a boy like Daniel, no matter how friendly he was, or how delicious he smelled. She resolved to put the nonsense out of her head. Next Saturday would be fun, even without Daniel and his lemony shampoo. Nora had lived in Nova Scotia all her life and never once been to Oak Island. Her parents weren't explorative types. No way was she wearing a bathing suit but she could manage a pair of shorts. Long ones, Bermuda shorts or clam diggers. Something to hide her thighs. Maybe she'd go back to Maggie's second hand store and see what she could find.

**

"What do you think of the guys?" Maggie asked Nora. "I mean, Daniel is totally hot, am I right?"

Nora bristled. The idea that Maggie Bench found Daniel O'Shea attractive made her feel lousy in her belly, although she couldn't exactly say why. What was it to her if Maggie and Daniel hooked up? And, why wouldn't they? Two of the prettiest people on campus were bound to gravitate towards each other. Plus, there was Maggie's promiscuity. Was Daniel the same? Nora frowned. She hadn't seen him around with any girls, but still...

"Alec is annoying," Nora stated, redirecting the conversation. Yes, Daniel O'Shea was totally hot. And smart, and kind, and a million other things a woman such as herself had no business fantasizing about. "Your typical dumb jock."

"He's adorable, though," Maggie said. "In that ambitious, puppy-dog way."

"But dumb as a post," Nora scoffed. "What is he even doing here? If he makes it past the first term, it'll be a miracle."

"I heard he's a good athlete."

"Obviously not that good if he couldn't crack the football team. I have a feeling the only thing that boy is good for is partying."

Maggie bit off a smile. She thought of Alec during frosh week – he'd gotten hold of a keg of beer somehow and was the center of attention. He'd stripped down to his boxers, dancing on a table, and Maggie was part of the crowd cheering him on. Of everyone in the group, Alec Yeats had the most potential for being fun. "What about Ashwin? Could you see yourself dating him?"

"Of course not," Nora scoffed. "I'm not here to date, I'm here to *learn*. Ashwin seems very nice and certainly intelligent. I think he's homesick, you can see it in his eyes."

"He's kind of shy, in a sweet way," Maggie said. "Notice how he never quite looks you in the eye?"

"He's probably afraid of all things female," Nora agreed and they both laughed.

"But I like the way he talks – his accent is sexy. Not much to look at, but if you closed your eyes..."

"Geez, Maggie, you have a one track mind."

Maggie grinned. "These are my 'fuck-years'. Gotta make the most of them."

"Your *what!?*"

"You know, your playing-around years, sowing your wild oats and all that. By time you hit twenty-five, it's too late, you know. You get too settled, in a serious relationship, career. Now is the time."

Damn, Nora thought. *I have totally missed my fuck-years.*

**

The male members of the Spirit Seeker Society were in the meeting room, studying. They didn't have the room booked but it was empty, and as Alec and Ashwin walked past, they'd noticed Daniel inside, sitting pensively at the long table, looking off into space. Ashwin dove right in, spreading his books out and opening his laptop. Alec had only his iPad, and was pretending to do research but was really playing a rousing game of Madden Football. Daniel had said he was studying but had no accoutrements. Just tapped his head and explained, "Just laying it out in my head. That's my process."

"What do you think of the girls?" Alec asked idly, flicking off his iPad with disgust. The game had ended and he'd lost. Geez, lately he couldn't even play a fictional game of football well. This place was messing with his mojo.

Daniel looked up. "Nora and Maggie? I think they're great. Why?"

"Maggie's a babe, a little dippy, but sweet. But the other one, Nora... she scares the shit out of me."

Daniel looked surprised. "Really? I don't see it. I don't find her scary at all."

"What do you think, Ash?" Alec asked. "Is Nora Berkowitz not the ugliest female you've ever seen? I mean, the nose on her! Geez, if I had a honker like that, I'd be standing in line at the plastic surgeon's office, begging to get it fixed. She looks like a witch."

Ashwin frowned. While it was true that Nora could not even be called a handsome woman, there was something about her he intrinsically liked. Yes, she was stern and bordering on cranky, but Ashwin suspected an intelligent mind. Nora Berkowitz seemed reliable and predictable – a very soothing combination. Especially in times like this, when Ashwin's entire world was askance.

It was Maggie who scared him. The look of a Hollywood starlet with her easy smile and quick wit, but she was too effervescent. Maggie stood so close that he was often forced to back up a few inches to maintain a comfortable body space, and she had the overly familiar habit of placing her hand on his arm when she addressed him. Ashwin Pawar had the sense that he could not trust Maggie Bench.

**

Maggie met a boy on Tuesday – a cute Asian fellow who was playing a guitar in the Quad. She spent

Tuesday evening at an off campus bar on Spring Garden Road. He was nineteen and Maggie had her fake ID, so getting served margaritas was no problem. One drink led to the next, and they staggered back to campus, arm-in-arm, trying to remember the words to 'Oh, Canada'. Each time they got to the second refrain they muffed up, which sent them into peals of laughter. Tommy also shared a room, so they hung a sock on the door to warn off his roommate, and continued on with the festivities.

On Wednesday night, Maggie met up with a different fellow – had drinks at a different bar, took in a free concert on the waterfront, shared a few joints, and wobbled back to campus. This guy had a single room, so no sock on the door was needed, and by Thursday morning, Maggie was bleary-eyed and sexually satisfied. Nora was asleep both nights when she slunk in and Maggie was secretly glad. She loved being with Nora – they were the campus misfits, but sometimes she just needed to be free and Nora was so tightly wound.

**

Nora heard Maggie come in both nights and feigned sleep. She kept her breathing deep and even, in case Maggie was listening, but Nora could tell from her stumbling state she wasn't. Where had she been? Was it with Kevin?

Nora had a secret of her own. She was kind of seeing Daniel.

After the Spirit Seeker Society's meeting on Monday, everyone left the room jabbering about the upcoming trip to Oak Island. They would need towels and sunscreen. Ashwin, in particular, seemed concerned about the logistics of it all, and Nora was grateful. It was nice to have someone else play stick-in-the-mud for a change. Usually Nora was stuck with the details, but since Ashwin stepped up, she was allowed to explore the novel experience of being carefree.

She'd noticed Daniel was still sitting at the table, brooding. Like before, he was wearing a simple white tee-shirt and jeans. He'd been quiet, tonight. Nora wondered if he was upset about being left out of the Oak Island trip. She knew firsthand how it felt to be excluded.

"Hey, Daniel. You okay?"

Daniel looked at her in surprise. It was like he'd been a million miles away in thought. "Sure."

"You look tired. A little. I mean, you look great – better than great. Just tired...." Her voice trailed off. Oh, fabulous. *She was babbling like an idiot.* Her cheeks flushed red. "Too bad you can't come with us. Maybe the group can come to one of your football games." *Ugh. Why had she said that?* She hated football. Sports in general, in fact.

"No worries," Daniel said.

Nora sat beside him. He really was the most exquisite creature. Nora was a gargoyle next to him. "We never asked how your spirit-search progress was going. What's the name of the girl you're trying to conjure? Lola?"

"Lila Rose."

"Any luck?"

"No. Lila Rose is proving to be maddeningly elusive."

"I did some ghost research," Nora said, shyly. Her voice was tentative and her shoulders curled defensively. At the first hint of Daniel's indifference, she was ready to bolt.
"Oh?"

"Yes. There's lots of data on the Internet. Most of it is stuff you see in the movies – cold spells, spirit orbs, but there are some other signs. Stranger things. Like foul odors."

"Really?" He looked interested. "What kind of odors?"

Nora shifted awkwardly. She was so tall, even sitting she had to bend her head slightly to meet his gaze. "It didn't elaborate, just mentioned foul odors. But it did say ghosts like the smell of lemons."

Daniel's mouth quirked. "I knew that." His grin was bashful. "Don't tell anyone, but I bought some lemon-scented soap from the drugstore, thought it might attract Lila Rose. Even used lemon shampoo. Doesn't seem to be helping, though."

She could smell the citrus on him. It was intoxicating. *My Heavens, what was happening to her? She got fluttery feelings around Daniel, around Maggie. Who was next? Ashwin and Alec? Her teachers? The janitor? Geez, she was a walking mass of sex hormones.* She felt the dampness between her legs and squirmed again. She was going to need another shower. Better make it a cold one. "Maybe Lila Rose doesn't like lemons?"

He looked interested. "Or maybe she doesn't like me."

"Or maybe she doesn't want to be disturbed."

"Or maybe there's no such thing as ghosts," he suggested. "Maybe I can bathe in lemons and the only thing I'll attract is fruit flies."

Nora thought of the apparition she saw at Madam Denicci's and shivered. A week ago, she would have agreed. Now she wasn't sure. She made her voice brisk, businesslike. "My research indicates there are five types of ghosts."

"Oh?" Daniel's eyebrow lifted slightly.

"Residual ghosts are the most common. Those are the saddest types of ghosts. Think of Heathcliff on the Moors, searching endlessly for his lost love. When someone dies suddenly or with great emotional angst their spirit may linger – and they are doomed to repeat the same pattern over and over. They might be walking through a garden, or down a flight of stairs, and the image plays endlessly."

"Like a film loop?"

"Exactly. It's important to note that you can't interact with a residual ghost because it isn't really there, just the representation. A local example of this is St Paul's Anglican Church – many people have seen an image in the window, it even shows up in photographs, and it reappears no matter how many times they replace the glass. It is believed that a priest was thrown out the window during the Halifax Explosion. Killed instantly, yet still his reflection remains."

"Yes, I've heard the story."

"Next, you have your *shadow people*. Those are figures that resemble a human and are often seen in corners or dark hallways, maybe standing over your bed. The distinctive thing about shadow people is their apparel, often wearing a top hat, fedora or cape. Imagine Phantom of the Opera or maybe Abraham Lincoln... Shadow people are a universal type of ghost – reported by all cultures and tribes, all walks of life."

"Equal opportunity haunting," Daniel suggested. Nora could tell he was intrigued and she felt emboldened to continue.

"Some believe that shadow people aren't really ghosts at all but perhaps aliens or even creatures from another dimension."

"That's disturbing."

"Isn't it, though? After seeing a shadow person, the viewer can feel a range of emotions, from dread, to fear, even severe depression. Some have said it was like seeing a harbinger of death."

"People *die* after seeing a shadow person?"

"Inconclusive. The suggestion was there. That brings us to *inhumane spirits* and *poltergeists* – worth a mention but not really relevant for our purposes."

Daniel leaned closer and again, Nora smelt the lemon. It was heady. She longed to bury her face deep into his hair, to wallow in it. *What was happening to her?* She cleared her throat and continued. "Inhuman spirits are demons, whose sole purpose appears to be conquering the will of those they possess. Think of '*The Exorcist*' and you get the picture – lots of noise, smashing of furniture, levitation, speaking in tongues, that sort of thing."

"Twisting heads, lots of vomit?"

Her mouth quirked. "Probably not, I suspect that made for exciting cinematography, if you go for that sort of thing. Effective though, it's the first thing that comes to mind when you think of '*The Exorcist*', isn't it? Then you have your poltergeist, which is characterised more as a playful entity. A prankster, if you will, moving objects, banging and crashing, generally making a nuisance of itself. Poltergeist means 'noisy ghost' in German, but some believe that a poltergeist isn't a ghost all, just a physical manifestation caused by adolescents, mainly females."

"Puts a new spin on teenage angst."

"Or a cop out. Gee, Mom, I didn't make this mess in my room, the poltergeist did."

"The perfect alibi."

"Exactly. Now, the last type of ghost is referred to as an *'intelligent spirit'*. This is the type of ghost we're seeking. They can also be called *'earthbound spirits'*, and for whatever reason, they choose to remain on earth. Maybe they have unfinished business, maybe they don't realize they're dead, maybe they just don't want to move on."

"Or maybe they can't move on," Daniel suggested.

"Right. The important thing to note is that intelligent spirits can communicate, can be seen, can even move objects."

There was a disturbance by the window. The curtains fluttered abruptly, and in her peripheral vision, Nora saw a shadow. Nothing substantial, and when she turned her face fully to the window, it had vanished.

Yet, against the window pane, remained the distinct impression of a handprint. Nora gasped and pointed, and they both moved quickly to the window. The handprint remained clear for several seconds before it dissipated.

Chills coursed down Nora's spine. The feeling of being watched returned tenfold. She waited for the lights to flicker but they remained bright.

"Maybe," Nora said slowly, "that was your ghost. Maybe Lila Rose is trying to tell us something."

CHAPTER SEVEN

*'Have you ever sensed that our soul is immortal and
never dies?' – Plato*

The workload at King's increased exponentially, and the students found themselves hard-pressed with the volume of reading. The FYP students had begun deciphering Plato's *Republic*, and heated conversations ensued in the cafeteria, the Quad and throughout dorms, debating Plato's question of whether *'a just man was any happier than an unjust man'*. The professor had asked them to define justice.

"What I don't get," Alec complained to Ashwin, "is this whole *forms* business. I can't wrap my head around it."

"The theory of forms is not that complex," Ashwin stated. "Plato argued that intellectual truth is more true than physical truth. He hypothesized that the creator, or God, if you will, is pure thought with no physical body yet he created the universe, and everything in it is mere copies of his original thought."

"Still not getting it."

Ashwin searched for an easier way to explain it. "Imagine something in your mind, anything. But it has to be completely original."

"Like what?"

"Make up a space creature. An alien."

"Like something in the bar scene from Star Wars?"

"No, something completely of your own making."

Alec closed his eyes. He tried to envision an original alien but he kept getting movie images. First the hideous creature that Sigourney Weaver chased in *Alien*, then the one from *Predator*. No, these weren't originals. Maybe friendlier? Now he could only think of *ET*. He sighed. He'd never been one for creativity. He was aware that Ashwin was watching him so he opened his eyes and said, "Ok, got it."

"Now," Ashwin said, "imagine your alien was standing here, right before us, that it was real. Plato's concept was that this alien would never be as pure or perfect as the one in your imagination, it would only be a copy."

"Like how a photocopy is never quite as clear as the original document?"

"Exactly," Ashwin beamed. "But keep in mind there was no original document, only the *idea* of one."

And, he was lost again. Jesus, he would *never* understand this stuff.

On a positive note, their ball hockey team was near the top of the rankings, even without the addition of Daniel, who politely thanked them for their invite but demurred as it would conflict with football practice. *And there it was,* Alec thought, *another stab in the gut.*

**

Ashwin was itchy to get back to the Old Burying Ground. He found the cemetery an ideal place to study. Somehow, sitting in a graveyard, looking at the markers of all those who had passed before him made everything seem trivial and transient. No matter what problems one had, either small or enormous, in a matter of decades, he too would meet this fate. Yes, he missed his family, but when confronted by the small amount of time one really had on this planet, it seemed ridiculous to waste precious time bemoaning it. Even Plato, a man who revolutionized philosophy and political theory, only lived a meagre eighty-one years.

Ashwin felt a presence and looked up. It was an orange tabby cat. "Hello," he said, softly. The cat rubbed itself against Robert Ross's tombstone. "Where did you come from? One of the surrounding houses, I imagine." He reached into his backpack and removed his tuna sandwich, offering a morsel of fish to the cat.

The cat was agreeable, lapped the tuna greedily, so Ashwin gave it another bit, then some more. By the time the sandwich was consumed, the relationship was solidified. "It seems, Major-General Ross, that we have company," Ashwin stated. The cat curled up on the tombstone, yawned, and napped in the luxurious warmth of the mid-September afternoon sun.

Across the graveyard, Ashwin noticed the ever-present caretaker, keeping to the far edges, and as always, going about his business as if Ashwin simply did not exist.

**

Nora was determined to make headway on finding her ghost. As usual, Pier 21 was crowded. There was a cruise ship in port and the museum was a popular place for tourists. The student rate was six dollars but the elderly ticket agent, recognizing Nora from before, let her go in free. "I remember, you're the girl from King's College doing the research project."

"Right," Nora said, surprised. People didn't usually remember her or offer her things for free. Ever.

"You were so disappointed that we closed at five, didn't give you enough time to look through the exhibits," he said.

"Right. Today, class finished early – I'll have two hours."

He stamped her hand. "Don't tell anyone," he winked. "We'll keep it between us King's students."

"You went to King's?" Nora asked in surprise.

"Sure. Graduated almost fifty years ago, 1965."

"Oh," she said in surprise. "Then you would have been gone by the time Lila Rose died."

His mouth thinned. "Yes, but my sister, Linda, knew her. Nasty business, that. Made a lot of news. It was rare for a student to die in those days, not like today with all those campus shootings and whatnot. Why do you ask?"

"Oh, no reason, I guess," Nora answered. She wasn't about to admit she was looking for ghosts. If he thought she was nutters, he wouldn't be letting her in for free, and six dollars was six dollars. Nora needed every cent she had.

"It was the strangest thing," the old man reminisced, his eyes glazing over as if he was back in time. "Never determined the cause of death. Room was locked, too, from the inside. They had to break down the door. No way could anyone have gotten out, unless it was the window, but it was shut, too. Pretty girl, Lila Rose, as I recall. Tiny little thing with dark hair."

Wonder if everyone would remember so well if Lila Rose had been ugly and tall? Nora thought.

"I guess it was the mystery that stuck with me," the man continued. "All those years, not knowing. Maybe natural causes, but I don't know... doesn't seem right...."

It was the perfect opening. "Are there any ghost stories at Pier 21?" Nora asked, keeping her voice casual.

His eyes shot back to her and he studied her, speculatively. "Nope. Why do you ask?"

"Oh, no reason. Just, there are so many ghost stories in Halifax that I thought this place might have a spooky tale or two."

"Nope. None I recall. Now, if you want a good ghost story, get yourself up to The Five Fishermen Restaurant, up on Argyle. That place is loaded with ghosts, as the stories go."

"Oh?"

"Sure. Used to be a funeral home, housed the bodies after the Titanic sank. Same for the Halifax Explosion. Why, that place has had more corpses grace its rooms than most graveyards." He leaned forward and crooked his finger. Nora leaned closer. "I hear the women's bathroom is particularly haunted." He had a funny gleam in his eye and Nora moved back quickly.

This old guy wasn't friendly. He was nothing but a creepy pervert.

**

The football team and cheerleaders rallied through the campuses of Dalhousie and King's, attempting to generate fan enthusiasm. For effect, they added a drummer and a trumpet blower, and the cheerleaders tossed flyers and mini footballs to anyone who would take them. A smattering of students joined the parade as it wound through the campuses and nearby streets like a messy, noisy snake. The football players wore full uniform, including helmets, and they looked like identical angry bees in their yellow and black jerseys.

"Which one is Daniel?" wondered Maggie, standing on the sidelines and waving.

"Dunno. They all look the same," Nora commented.

"What number is he?"

"No idea."

"Geez," Maggie said. "We're kind of crappy friends." A husky football player broke ranks and swooped Maggie into his arms and the crowd whopped with laughter as he carried her along in the parade. Maggie did not seem to mind, even when her skirt rode up and flashed her undies at the crowd.

Nora scowled. She was absolutely certain that no virile, faceless dumb jock would spontaneously scoop her up. Never in a million years.

Oh, but she wished someone would.

She raised her hand over her eyes, visor-style, scanning the players for Daniel. From the corner of her eye, she caught sight of her dorm window. The curtains flickered and she saw a distinct silhouette.

Someone was in her room.

**

Maggie didn't make it back to campus until almost midnight. The football rally finished up at Wickwire field where free hot dogs and sodas were served. Her capturer set her down gently on the turf and removed his helmet. She could tell he was black from the skin color of his arms, but what surprised her was how gorgeous he was. Simply scrumptious with puppy dog eyes and a large smile that took up half his face, and lips that Maggie could lose herself in.

Maggie felt the stirrings of lust. She'd never had a black lover before.

His name was Tyrone. He thanked Maggie for being a good sport and Maggie thanked him for being so gentle. "You could have been a little rougher," she teased. "Sometimes I like it that way."

Tyrone smiled even wider.

He showed her the team locker room and suggested they go for drink at *Your Father's Moustache* on Spring Garden Road, a few blocks away. They ate roasted vegetable Panini's and sweet potato fries, and Tyrone told Maggie he was in third year, working towards his bachelor of science. "I plan to study medicine," Tyrone said.

"Huh," Maggie teased. "I thought football players were supposed to be dumb."

Tyrone grinned. "That's what I thought about blond girls."

"Touché," laughed Maggie.

He told her about his assignment for molecular biology and she told him about Plato and Virgil, and they both agreed each other's classes were like speaking another language. Then Maggie told Tyrone about the Spirit Seeker Society and about the ghost at Madam Denicci's.

"No way," Tyrone said, mouth hanging open.

"Way," Maggie nodded. "I swear."

"This I gotta see," Tyrone said. So they took a taxi to the Hydrostone but found the psychic was closed for business. "Guess she doesn't do evenings," Tyrone said, clearly disappointed.

"No matter," Maggie said. "Ghosts don't keep office hours. We just need to find her. Now, if I was a ghost, where else would I go?" She closed her eyes and concentrated.

Nothing happened.

They strolled the wide streets of the Hydrostone hand in hand. The sun was just starting to set and Tyrone suggested they pick up a bottle of wine and drink it in the park.

"Great idea," Maggie said. They entered the liquor store five minutes before closing time, chose

Chianti with a screw top and asked for two paper cups at Tim Hortons. By the time the bottle was almost finished, they'd rolled under the canopy of a large umbrella tree, giggling, and Tyrone showed Maggie his best moves off the gridiron.

The sex was phenomenal. Maggie's eyes rolled back in her head, seeing the last vestiges of daylight filter through the dense branches of the tree. Had she kept her eyes open, she may have noticed the forlorn expression of the fortune teller's resident ghost, watching them.

**

Nora frowned. Her dorm room was locked and empty. Everything looked normal. Untouched. Well, hard to tell from Maggie's side where clothing and textbooks sprang forth like weeds. Nora absently began tidying, sorting dirty clothes from clean, sniffing occasionally to be sure. When everything was sorted into two piles, she transferred the clean pile into the closet cubby. Here, more mess sprang, and Nora debated whether to tidy it as well. Would Maggie mind? Nora wouldn't like anyone poking through her own private belongings.

She could leave the pile on the bed but Maggie would likely flop down, sending everything flying. Nora had learned this from experience. So, she opened the cubby door, intending to set the clothes inside, determined not to snoop.

Ah, a giant box of condoms. Figures, Nora thought distastefully. *Hmmm, I wonder.....* Nora slipped out one of the packets, opened it up and peered inside. Like a water balloon, only greasier. *I wonder what this would feel like, inside me?* She lay on Maggie's

86

bed and closed her eyes, trying to imagine it. *What if Daniel put it on? What would that be like?*

The cubby door slammed of its own accord.

Nora's eyes flew open and she frowned. She slipped the condom into her pocket and stood, closing the cubby firmly, hearing the latch click. She flicked on the desk lamp and walked over to the window, peering into the Quad below. This was where she'd seen the figure standing, she was certain of it.

Could it have been a trick of light?

The lamp clicked off.

Frowning, Nora left the window and turned the light back on.

It stayed off.

She tried the overhead light.

It, too, stayed off.

A power failure? She walked to the window again and saw lights in the other dorm rooms. Electricity seemed okay.

The cubby door flew open. The neatly piled clothes tumbled out, spilling onto the floor.

"Lila?" Nora whispered. "Lila Rose? Is that you?"

The air felt heavy, oppressive. Nora felt a stab of irrational fear. *I've got to get out of here,* she thought. There was a rattle at the door and she looked at it wildly.

As at Madam Denicci's, Nora's legs were leaden and it was difficult to move. She stood and forced her feet forward. It was like walking through quicksand and she panicked, felt her heart race. The room was small and the door was almost within arm's length but it felt so far. Her feet struggled to cross the floor, she was only managing inches.

"Stop this," she hissed, talking to no one. "If you're trying to frighten me, it's working. But I don't want to be frightened. I want to see you. I want to help you move on, Lila Rose. I know it's you. I demand you stop this nonsense and let me go."

The air lightened and her feet felt normal. Nora took another look around the room: nothing. No unearthly spirits. She took in a great gulp of air and swung open the door.

Daniel.

He was on the other side, hand raised as if to knock, surprise registering on his face. "What are you doing here?" he asked.

"This is my room," Nora said. "Maggie and I switched." Then comprehension: if he wasn't looking for her, what was *he* doing here? She asked him as much.

"Looking for Lila Rose," Daniel said. "This was her room."

Nora stared. "Really?" She held the door wide open. "Well, I do believe she might be here."

Daniel came in, his eyes narrowed speculatively. "Why is it so dark?"

Nora shrugged. "The lights lost power."

"Try again."

Nora flipped the switch and the little room was bathed in light.

"You're going to think I'm making this up," Nora said. "But something weird was going on, I swear. The cubby door was banging – all those clothes fell out."

Daniel put his hands on his hips and looked around. Nora surreptitiously toed the box of condoms under the pile of clothing.

"Mind if I stay with you for a bit? See if Lila Rose comes back?"

Nora's heart skipped a beat. "Sure, no problem. Make yourself comfortable."

Daniel sat on Nora's bed and she took a seat on Maggie's, pushing the clothes to one side. Out of nervous habit she began folding them again, and then stopped herself, especially as Daniel's eyes settled on a pair of Maggie's tiny panties. "I saw her," she began, tentatively. "Or, at least I thought saw I her – in the window – during the football rally." Nora stopped, aware of how ridiculous she sounded.

Daniel didn't answer, just continued to look around the room. The moment stretched and time passed. Both remained silent. The room remained still. A thin beat of music wafted through the walls; someone had their speakers turned up. Nora could hear low mumblings of words, snippets of laughter. Someone in the Quad hollered.

Daylight faded and Nora drifted off, her back against the wall, Maggie's belongings spread about her and an excruciatingly handsome boy staring at her in the bunk across. When she awoke, the room was pitch black, her neck was god-awful stiff and Daniel was gone.

It wasn't until the next morning she noticed a handprint on the window pane, underscored with feathery writing: *beware.*

CHAPTER EIGHT

*'Greater love has no one than this, that he lay down his
life for his friends'*
– The Bible, John 15:13

It took the better part of an hour to drive to Oak Island, plus another fifteen minutes to pick up a bucket of chicken, soda and a proper amount of road trip junk food. Conversation centered around this week's lectures, the amount of reading required, and the nightly dart tournament held in the Wardroom. The boys told the girls about the ball hockey intramural and suggested they join. "Teams are coed," Alec said, "but there seems to be more guys than girls. We need at least two girls for every team."

"Sounds like a blast," said Maggie.

"I don't do sports," said Nora.

The conversation turned to ghostly apparitions, both in the dorm room and at Madam Denicci's.

"It might be a prank," Ashwin suggested. "Our goal isn't secret. I've had other students question me about our society. It seems we've created a small buzz around campus. Perhaps someone is having us on."

"I know what I saw. That ghost-woman was definitely there. And besides, why would a reputable business get caught up in a campus prank?" Maggie was adamant.

"It *could* have been a fake," Nora said slowly. "How legitimate can a psychic really be? The whole thing screams *'fraud'*. And, what do we really know about Madam Denicci, anyway? Maybe it's time to do a background check on her."

"What about the stuff in our room?" Maggie asked, pushing her windblown hair from her eyes. It framed her face like a wild, golden halo. It was officially the first day of autumn but still felt like summer. The borrowed car had no air-conditioning so they kept the windows down, and were forced to yell to be heard over the roar of the highway. The view was breathtaking: craggy bays and quaint fishing villages – this was the Nova Scotia shown on postcards. And, everywhere, the sparkling blue ocean stretching to infinity. In Nova Scotia, one was never far from the sea.

"There's probably a logical explanation," Ashwin suggested, his British-Indo accent pleasing to the ear. "Maggie, according to Nora, your belongings were piled very high – no wonder the cubby door fell open. The sheer volume was no match for the hinges."

"And the figure in the window?"

"Trick of light, perhaps?"

Nora shook her head. But Ashwin was right – everything could be explained. She'd only seen the figure for the fleetingness of moments. It could have been an optical illusion. She could have imagined it.

"I am still hog-bozzled that you two are living in Lila Rose's room," Ashwin stated. "That is a staggering coincidence."

Nora thought of the machinations that Maggie went through to switch rooms. Was it? Were they making poor choices like the psychic warned? Or was this some colossal, elaborate joke with Nora destined to bear the brunt? She'd seen the horror movie *Carrie*, she knew how these things went.

"Actually," Maggie was saying, "it does make sense. No wonder those other girls were so happy to switch rooms. Our room is *haunted*."

Said aloud like that, on this brilliant sunny day surrounded by beaches and ocean, it seemed absurd and they all laughed. Even Nora.

"What does Daniel think?" Ashwin wondered.

"Don't know. He didn't say much. But he seemed keen to believe. Hold up, Alec, there's the turn off."

"Oak Island Inn, gotta be the right place."

But when they got there, and asked for directions at the Inn, they realized they were not. Oak Island was a private island and not accessible to the public. "There are private tours," the desk clerk said and checked her computer. "Next one is in a couple of weeks."

Alec looked crestfallen.

"Geez, Alec, you dumb-ass, didn't you check your facts before we came all this way?" Nora asked with disgust.

"It never occurred to me. I mean, the place is famous. It's even featured in Assassin's Creed 3... It's a video game," he explained.

"Well, there's a definitive source. Where else did you gather research, Wikipedia?" Nora flung up her hands. "So, what now? Turn around and go home?"

"There's still the beach," Maggie said. "No point ruining the whole day."

"We'll sneak in," Alec said. He wasn't willing to give up, not quite yet. The *dumb-ass* comment stung. Truth was, he hadn't done any research – was just relying on memory from his old school project. And even then, his mom had done most of the work.

Ashwin frowned. "What do you mean?"

"Look, the island is connected by a causeway – it was built to transport the crane for digging. There's just a small gate – we couldn't get the car past, but what's to stop us from walking in?"

"Trespassing? That's against the law," Ashwin said nervously. "If we get caught, I could be deported. I'm here on a student visa – I'm not allowed to get into trouble."

"Maybe Ashwin could stand guard while the rest of us check it out?" Alec suggested. "Ash, you could be the lookout. If anyone comes, call my cell."

Ashwin stepped back. "That sounds like a very poor plan. Perhaps we should come back when there is a proper tour."

"I'm with Ashwin on this," Nora said.

"Oh, you two are a couple of sticks in the mud. Where's your sense of adventure?" Maggie scoffed. "We came all this way – are you going to let a little gate and a warning sign stop you?"

So it was settled: Maggie and Alec would see if they could walk past the gate undetected, and Nora and Ashwin would act as lookouts.

**

"Tell me," Ashwin asked Nora, "what do you know of this Money Pit? Other than it being featured in a video game," he quipped, and Nora smiled despite her mood.

They had settled against a log on a small, sandy beach. It was low tide, and the waves lapped languidly along the shoreline. A tiny pair of pipers hopped along, pecking indiscriminately at the sand.

"Well, if you grow up in Nova Scotia, you grow up hearing about Oak Island and the Money Pit. It's the world's longest running treasure hunt, a Two hundred year old mystery," Nora said, squinting into the sun, trying to remember the facts. "There's an elaborate shaft with multiple layers, and despite many attempts, no one has ever gotten to the bottom.

Lots of theories – everyone has a hypothesis but no answer."

The story went like this: in 1795, a teenager named Daniel McGinnis saw mysterious lights coming from Oak Island. At that time, there was no land bridge, so he rowed out to investigate. He found a circular depression and started poking around. He discovered a layer of flagstones a few feet down, and enlisted the help of friends and started digging. At ten feet, they located a layer of logs. They dug as far as thirty feet, finding more layers of logs at ten foot intervals, and then they gave up, lacking the equipment to explore deeper.

Over the next two hundred years, various individuals and corporations would attempt to learn the secret of the Money Pit. Every twenty years or so, another group would try their luck. More layers were discovered. At forty feet, lay charcoal. At fifty feet was a layer of putty. And, more intriguing, at sixty feet lay a thick swath of coconut fiber, a material not found within 2400 kilometres of Nova Scotia.

At approximately eighty feet lay the most perplexing layer of all: a stone tablet inscribed in code. When deciphered, it read: *'forty feet below, two million pounds lie buried'.*

What did this mean? Who buried it? Theories abounded. Could it be the pirate Blackbeard's ill-gotten booty? He'd been known to sail the area and had famously boasted he hid treasure *'where none but Satan and myself can find it'.* Or, perhaps it contained Marie Antoinette's jewels – a maid escaped Versailles with important treasures and certainly the structure bore traces of French design. Some expressed it might hold looted cache from the Crusades – namely, the Holy Grail and the Ark of the

Covenant. This speculation was fueled by the mysterious departure of eighteen French galleys in 1307. Regardless, whatever lay beneath remains untouched to present day despite millions of dollars spent searching for the secret.

"What was below the tablet layer?" Ashwin asked, intrigued.

"That's where it really gets interesting. After the tablet, excavators were excited to find a layer of oak chests and loose metal – exactly what treasure hunters hoped to find. But the search was booby trapped, exposing the first of several flood channels. As they dug deeper, the pit began to fill with seawater."

"So, how deep did they go?"

"I believe they got 235 feet with a tube, collecting samples. Oh, and listen to this: near the bottom, they found human remains. How did those get there? Were they sacrificial? The whole thing is creepy, mystery upon mystery." Nora lowered her voice for effect, surprised to realize how much she was enjoying herself. Ashwin was an easy companion. His gentle demeanor and quiet manner were soothing. "Plus, there are clues on the island itself, some cone-shaped rocks inscribed with the same symbols as the tablet – when the lines are connected, it forms a giant cross, which supports the Knights Templar theory. One of its members built a castle in New Ross, not far from here."

"And people died?"

"Six in all. Legend has it that treasure won't be found until seven lives are lost. Another says the treasure won't be found until all the oak trees disappear from Oak Island – currently a single oak tree remains."

Ashwin shivered despite the warmth of the day. "Do you believe that?"

"Of course not," Nora said, shrugging. A cloud floated over the sun and blocked it from view, lowering the temperature dramatically. "Do you?"

Ashwin didn't answer. He stared at Oak Island. It was quiet and appeared uninhabited. "I wonder if they reached the Money Pit, yet? I hope they're careful."

Nora scoffed. "Those two wing-nuts? I doubt it. Knowing Maggie, they're probably having sex on the beach."

**

"Which ghost are you hoping to connect with?" Maggie asked Alec. They hadn't spoken much before and, of all the group members, Alec remained the most distant to her. She was glad to have this time alone to get to know him; he was actually pretty cute.

"The guy who died first, in 1890-something." Alec visualized his younger self standing in front of the class, giving an oral report. The facts were coming back to him. "Maynard Kaiser. That's it, I remember because it sounded like a sandwich: mayonnaise on a Kaiser roll. Geez, imagine being saddled with the name Maynard." Alec said derisively. "Anyway, Old Mayonnaise fell to his death, or drowned... or something. Hey, Maggie?"

"Yeah?"

"Did you really see a ghost at the fortune teller's or were you just shittin' us?"

"We really saw it. I swear."
"Were you scared?"

"No. Well, maybe a little freaked. She seemed harmless, though." Maggie frowned. "Truthfully, I was more scared of the Tarot reading. The cards were harsh. Said we were making bad choices."

Alec grinned. "Like sneaking onto a restricted island and searching for ghosts?"

Maggie nodded. "Yeah, sort of like that."

They rounded the corner and came to a look off.

"Hey, I think that might be it," Alec said, pointing down the hill.

"Look, there's someone down there."

"What are they doing? Digging?"

"No, just standing there. Oh, crap, they see us. Should we take off?"

"No way," Maggie said. She adjusted her tee-shirt so it rode a little lower in the cleavage and higher on the stomach, exposing the twinkling diamond of her belly-piercing. She exuded confidence. "Let's introduce ourselves."

Alec halted. His earlier bravado had worn off. He was uncomfortably aware that it was very secluded here. And, they *were* trespassing. "Wait up, Mags. I'm not sure this is a good idea."

She frowned. "Why? Worse they can do is tell us to leave. C'mon, stop being such a baby."

The feeling of malevolence increased. Alec had the urge to run. They had closed the gap; the two men were close enough to call to. Alec couldn't quite make out their faces but their body language looked hostile. The men were standing still, watching and waiting.

Still, Alec hesitated. "I don't know. I have a bad feeling." He swallowed, his Adam apple bobbling convulsively.

"Do you want to find your ghost or not? C'mon, Alec." She strode ahead.

The feeling stayed with him. *They should not be here.* It was as if the words were whispered directly into his ear.

**

"Tell me about India," Nora said to Ashwin.

"What do you want to know?"

"What's it like? You must be homesick."

You have no idea, he thought. They had kicked off their shoes and Ashwin stretched his brown toes in the warm sand. He was excruciatingly tired. Last night brought about his worst bout of insomnia yet, and he hoped the sea air and exercise would allow him to sleep tonight. "India is half a world away," he said, finally, "and sometimes I feel as if I have arrived on another planet. Only the ocean feels familiar, but the color is the wrong shade of blue, so even it feels unfamiliar. And the ocean is so cold here, I feel as if an iceberg will come floating past any minute."

Nora smiled. The water *was* frigid. Perfect for growing lobster – less so for human bathers. "How did you end up here? In Nova Scotia, of all the places you could have chosen in the world?"

"It was my father's decision. He felt it was important for me to conduct my education abroad. He considered England and America, but chose Halifax as he felt the atmosphere would suit me."

"And does it?"

Ashwin considered. He looked around at the craggy shoreline, the many green islands dotting the large bay. Compared with the color and crowds of India, this seemed like a wilderness frontier. Instead of scents like jasmine and curry, he smelled only the clear, salt air. He looked at the tall, awkward woman sitting next to him. "Yes," he said, his teeth showing whitely. "It suits me. Papa was right."

"I think it takes tremendous courage."

"Do you?" Ashwin asked, wondering. The real courage would have been in defying his father.

"Sure. I've never even been outside Nova Scotia. Say, how are you making out with your own ghost hunt? Any progress?"

Ashwin smiled depreciatingly. "None, although I've recently made a very good friend in a stray tabby. She seems to love the tuna I bring her from the cafeteria each day. At first, she was aloof but now she comes running. And the caretaker – I do believe he is warming up to me. The other day, I could have sworn he actually looked in my direction."

"Tell me, do you believe in ghosts?" Nora asked, her face growing serious.

"No."

"Then why spend so much time at the Old Burying Ground?"

How could he explain it? "There is a sense of tranquility. Being surrounded by thousands of souls who passed before me puts my life in perspective. I read their tombstone inscriptions and I wonder: *Who were they?* They were real people at one time, with families and hopes and fears, not so very different from us. It makes me question: what is my purpose? Why am I here when I am fated to join them in such a short time?"

"Perhaps you are here for a grander purpose. Maybe Ashwin Pawar exists to do great deeds."

He thought of Major-General Robert Ross, who existed only thirty-eight years. Yet he lived those years gloriously: heroically and patriotically. Fighting wars and commanding troops. "More likely," Ashwin said, tossing a pebble into the ocean and watching the small ripple fade into nothingness, "I shall be like this stone. Only one tiny pebble in the vast sea."

**

When they reached the Money Pit, the two men they'd spied from the top of the hill had disappeared. "Where did they go?" Maggie wondered.

"To call the police, probably," Alec said. "Let's not linger. Take a look, snap some photos and get the hell out of here." The ominous feeling hadn't left Alec. He was edgy, nervous. And it wasn't just the trespassing and isolation that left him feeling like this. It was... creepy.

"Not much to look at," Maggie said. "Just a hole and this crappy fencing."

"It wouldn't keep anyone out," Alec agreed, looking over his shoulder. "Maybe deer, but not people."

"Should we go in? See if we can climb into the Money Pit?"

No!

"Maybe we'll find the treasure," Maggie joked. "Hey, I'm going in. Take my picture, will you?"

His mouth went dry and the words came out as a whisper. *"Maggie, no!"*

"Geez, you're as chicken as the other two. I wish Daniel was here, he wouldn't be afraid of ghosts."

"I'm not afraid of ghosts," Alec said, "but I am afraid of falling. That pit is over two hundred feet deep."

"So? I'll be careful." She was already straddling the fence. "Do you feel a ghostly presence?" Maggie teased. She flipped her other leg over and she was inside. Alec felt his heart pound erratically as she stood over the pit, peering. "Wow, it's dark in there." She activated the flashlight app on her iPhone and

100

directed the beam. "Hellloooo, down there," she called into the hole. "Anyone down there?"

The foreboding grew until it almost choked Alec. His feet were leaden and he couldn't speak. The hairs on his neck and arms were standing at attention. *Couldn't Maggie feel it?* She was directly over the pit, looking in, climbing down. "Stop," he tried to say, but the words came out in a croak. She was all the way in now, only the top of her blond head poked out. Alec tried to move his feet but it was as if they were mired in quicksand. His nostrils were assailed with a rotten, fetid smell – where moments before had been only the strong, briny scent of the tide. *Skunk?* No, worse.

Maggie popped her head up like a mole and scowled at him. "Are you coming or not?"

He opened his mouth and only squeaks came out.

"Wow, it's crazy in here," Maggie said, her head disappearing again. Her words drifted up, hollow sounding. "Watch your footing; it would be so easy to slip. Hey, how did you say that guy Maynard died? Falling to his death? Yeah, I could totally see that happening. Whoops, almost lost it there. Hey Alec," she called, her voice growing fainter. "Are you coming or not?"

Alec looked around, wildly. Even his head felt difficult to move, and his eyes blinked rapidly. A movement on the hill – two figures... the same two they'd seen on the beach? They were on the hill now, watching. The same hill Maggie and he had been on earlier, now their positions reversed. What were they doing? If only he could turn his head all the way, but it was immobile. His eyes could only see so much. They were throwing their heads back and.... laughing?

And, then, they simply disappeared.

Alec broke free all at once. He found his feet moving, his arms waving, his mouth working manically. "Maggie," he yelled. "Get out of there! Run!" He started sprinting down the beach, in the opposite direction of the two figures on the hill. Without conscious thought, he fled in an all consuming panic. In a move that would later fill him with embarrassment and shame, Alec left the pretty, blond-haired girl alone in the Money Pit.

CHAPTER NINE

*'Of all creatures that breath and move upon the earth,
nothing is bred that is weaker than man' – Homer*

On Sunday, a hurricane warning was issued for Nova Scotia, with emphasis on the Halifax metro area. Hurricanes were rare this far north, usually arctic air and cooling sea prevented storm systems from travelling this far up the coast. But this year, the unusually hot summer kept the Atlantic Ocean temperatures warmer than average, and this particular storm, instead of peeling outwards at the Carolina's, continued its swath of destruction up the coast with an eye on Halifax. The morning started clear and calm, but clouds crept ominously from the south by late afternoon. Due to the impending storm, the football game was rescheduled from two o'clock to noon, and the time change was not beneficial to the visiting team: Dalhousie Tigers were mauled 38 to 7 by the Prince Edward Island Panthers, and the return bus trip was a muted affair.

Alec Yeats sustained a sprained ankle on his mad dash from Money Pit to mainland. Maggie appeared fifteen minutes behind him, cool and collected, appearing magically like a sun kissed mermaid with her flowing ringlets and shimmering tanned body. *Was her skin naturally iridescent or was it from a sparkling body lotion?* Nora wondered, catching her breath.

"Thanks for waiting, Dickwad," Maggie said, only half joking.

Alec closed his mouth mutinously. He would not admit he was frightened. Or, that he thought the two figures on the hillside were ghosts. It seemed ridiculous now that he was away from it.

"I told you not to go in that pit," he said. His ankle, twisted when he fell over a protruding rock, hurt like a bugger.

"Whatever," Maggie said, flipping her hair back. "I got pictures for you." She looked at her phone and frowned. "Oh, damn. They didn't turn out – too dark in there, I guess. Look at this – what are these weird spots?" She showed them the image – a series of small, round orbs lit up the bottom left hand corner.

"Doesn't matter," Alec said defiantly. "This whole ghost thing is stupid. I quit."

Nora looked at him sharply. "What do you mean, you quit? *You can't quit.* This is a mandatory assignment."

His mouth quivered and he looked like he might cry. "I don't care – ow! Holy shit, Nora, that hurts! Stop poking me."

Nora released his ankle. "It doesn't look broken. Can you walk?"

"Yeah," Alec said, standing and testing his weight. "Let's get the *eff* out of here." He cautioned a glance back at Oak Island. It looked quiet, serene. He grimaced. "Someone else has to drive – this is my pedal foot."

"I'll do it," Maggie volunteered.

"No!" The others all said in unison, and Maggie stepped back.

"I don't have an international driver's permit," Ashwin stated.

"I'll drive," Nora said, taking the keys.

"Can you drive a stick?" Alec asked. It was his friend's car, and if anything happened to it, it was his ass in a sling.

"Of course I can," Nora barked. "What do you think I am, an imbecile? Toss me the keys."

"Are we still going to the beach?" Maggie asked. She sounded like a little girl whose party had been ruined.

"No."

"You guys suck," Maggie stated to no one in particular.

**

By the time the bus deposited the football players in the Dalhousie parking lot, the storm clouds had picked up serious attitude. The wind hadn't started yet, just the occasional gust to test things out, and everyone milled excitedly. Daniel looked into the Quad – students were having a storm rally. He decided to check out the girls' room – perhaps the ramped electrical energy of the upcoming hurricane might encourage ghostly activity? He didn't really believe it but he was desperate to make contact with Lila Rose.

He'd joked to the others that ghosts didn't exist, but Daniel knew the truth. It was no accident he was in the Spirit Seeker Society. Lila Rose had information and he desperately needed it.

The girls had given him permission to enter their room and Maggie left him a key. They were slated to spend the full day at Oak Island but with the impending storm, he suspected they would return early. If he wanted to do this alone, he would have to make it fast.

He could tell with a glance which side was Nora's: spartan and prim, the plain black bedspread with its corners tucked in army-style precision. In contrast, Maggie's side was a whirlwind – much like her blond ringlets. The duvet was squashed in the corner, a plethora of pillows lined the wall – clothes and makeup and books were strewn haphazardly both on the bed and around it. Daniel smiled. Maggie was the essence of a free spirit. He leaned over one of the pillows – a furry one – and breathed in. Yup, Maggie.

He sat on Maggie's bed, feeling awkward. He looked around the empty room and cleared his throat. "Lila? Please show yourself, I know you're afraid but you needn't be. I just want to talk."

No answer.

"Please, Lila." He took a deep breath. "I need to see you."

The room remained silent and still.

"Lila Rose," Daniel said, trying to remain calm as his frustration grew. "You are as much a coward in death as you were in life."

**

The first fat drops of rain had started to fall and the wind was picking up as Nora turned the car into the King's parking lot. "Good thing we didn't go to the beach," she muttered.

"It would have been epic," Maggie disagreed. "The beach is awesome when a storm hits."

"You're crazy," Alec said. But he smiled. The further they got away from Oak Island, the more foolish he felt.

"Come on, Alec," Ashwin said, holding out his arm. "Let's get you to the campus medic, you need your ankle examined."

"It's okay, now," Alec said. "See? I can stand on it. Just a little swelling. Let's hit the cafeteria – I'm hungry. Wow, look at all the students in the Quad. Wonder what's happening? Looks like a party." He turned to a passing student. "Hey, what's going on?"

"Haven't you heard, dude? We're getting a hurricane! Sweet, eh?"

Maggie jumped up and down, clapping her hands. "Oooh, that's totally awesome. She followed the guy into the Quad to join the festivities, leaving the other three behind without a backward glance.

Ashwin frowned, looking at the dancing students, the revelry. "A hurricane? Is this not something to be alarmed at? Should people not be taking precautions, boarding windows, gathering supplies, that sort of thing?"

"Only the smart ones," Nora mumbled.

"Don't worry," Alec said. "It won't amount to much – it'll be all bark and no bite. C'mon, Ash – I'm really starving here. Help me walk to the cafeteria."

**

The hurricane struck at midnight. It was classified as a borderline category two, with wind speeds clocked at 160 kilometres on George's Island in the Halifax harbor. The city sustained widespread damage. Uprooted trees, buckled boardwalks on the waterfront, broken windows and damaged roofs, plus extensive power outages. The storm passed out to sea by daybreak, but classes were cancelled.

The stone walls of King's College remained unscathed but the campus grounds were plastered with shredded leaves and twigs. The inner courtyard was relatively protected, but the outer walls were another story, with century old trees snapped like twigs. The large deciduous trees, still in full-leaf, had come crashing down; pulling up chunks of concrete sidewalk, exposing roots.

"I'm going downtown to explore," Maggie said, stripping off her tank top and sorting through her piles of clothes, naked except for a pair of boy boxers.

Nora tried not to stare. "Do you think that's wise? Power lines are down all over the place. Police have asked people to remain at home."

"C'mon, Nora. It'll be a blast."

Nora yawned. "You think everything's a blast. Nah, I think I'll stay here and catch up on my reading – get a start on this week's assignments."

Maggie jumped on Nora's bed. "C'mon, Nora! How often do we get a hurricane? Almost never! Last one was ten years ago. What harm can there be?"

There was a sudden crack and both girls jumped. The window pane shattered and glass flew inwards.

"That's strange," Nora said, jumping up. She put her shoes on and carefully walked over to the window, looking out. "Huh, must have been weakened by the hurricane. That's weird, looks like ours is the only broken one."

**

Ashwin had slept poorly. The hurricane had enough velocity that the wind kept him awake. His room faced outwards and he could see a small triangle of the watery inlet of the Northwest Arm. It was eerily quiet outside – usually by this time, the morning rush-hour was upon them and the streets were congested. Now, not a single car drove past.

**

Alec's ankle throbbed painfully. The bruise extended from his toes to mid-calf and he wiggled his toes experimentally. Swelling seemed to be the main issue, so he popped four Advil and wrapped it tightly in tensor bandage. As an athlete, this kind of injury was commonplace – he'd be back to fighting form in a few days.

He could tell the power was off but hopefully the campus kitchen had generator power. He was starving, again, and a bowl of cold cereal wasn't going to cut it.

**

Daniel paced the second floor study room where the Spirit Seeker Society usually met. This part of the campus was morbidly quiet. With classes cancelled for the day, students had no reason to venture into the upper floors of Prince Hall. The lights remained off, and even though morning had arrived with clear blue sky and a brilliant sun, the room remained dim.

Despite spending hours yesterday trying to reach Lila Rose, he had failed. He would have to come up with another method to lure his reluctant ghost.

**

This time, Maggie's ghost found her. She had planned to jog the waterfront, but police cars blocked her route, cutting off traffic and passengers alike from the downed power lines. Maggie had a great deal of pent up energy and a vigorous run seemed the perfect vent.

The post hurricane air was cooler – the heat and humidity of the past few weeks had finally broken. She jogged with no particular destination, just zigzagged through the city streets, going in the direction her feet took her. The streets were ominously quiet – very few cars, lots of emergency vehicles, and a few fellow joggers and dog walkers, out to explore the aftermath of the storm.

The city felt cleansed and Maggie ran with pure enjoyment. It felt good to leave everything behind – the crowded campus, academia, even her friends. When she finally felt winded, she stopped and took stock of her surroundings, a little surprised to find herself in the Hydrostone district. She took a seat on a park bench, not too far from the umbrella tree where she'd enjoyed Tyrone. She was thirsty, and she was lamenting the lack of foresight to bring water – everything was closed. Even Tim Horton's. It appeared the power outage was city wide.

She was contemplating knocking on someone's door and asking for a glass of water when the ghost-lady appeared beside her.

"Holy shit," Maggie said. "You scared me."

"Sorry. I don't have much practice with this sort of thing. You're the only person who's seen me since... well, since... I died."

"When was that?"

"1917. It feels like yesterday – time is different here."

"I knew it!" Maggie said. Her initial fright had passed and she forced herself to remain calm, to keep her body still. The last thing she wanted was to frighten the ghost. "I knew you were from the Halifax Explosion. I could tell by your dress – it totally fits the time period."

The ghost frowned, looking down at herself. Her image was wavery – she was not as clear as in Madam Denicci's reading room – but still clear enough that Maggie could make out her expression. "Oh, no, dear. I didn't die in the explosion. I was murdered."

**

Ashwin made his way down to the Old Burying Ground, shocked to see the destruction on the streets of Halifax. Mostly uprooted trees and debris, but he passed three separate incidents where trees had fallen onto cars, crushing them. Roof shingles and debris lay everywhere, plus occasional patches of broken window glass.

The graveyard was in poor shape. Several trees had uprooted here as well, disturbing the burial plots around them. Many of the tombstones had fallen or tilted. The front gate remained locked, and he looked through them, chagrined. In the far corner, he could see the elderly caretaker. As always, he kept his face turned from Ashwin.

Something nudged his foot and he stepped back, in alarm, half expecting a dislodged hand from an overturned grave to reach through the fence and grab him. It was the orange tabby – looking for a handout.

"Hello, Billi," he said, using the Hindi word for cat. "I'm terribly sorry but no treats today. I am glad to see you weathered the storm safely."

The orange tabby meowed and slipped through the wrought iron fencing, heading in the direction of Robert Ross's grave. It turned once to look at Ashwin, twitching its tail, its green eyes enigmatic, as if to say, "Well, are you coming or aren't you?"

**

Alec sat in the cafeteria and scowled. His worst fears were confirmed: there was no hot food. He looked at the bowl of Raisin Bran with disdain. Rumor swirled that power was out for much of Nova Scotia. He wouldn't be able to find a decent breakfast *anywhere* this morning. *It better be restored by afternoon,* he thought. He had a full complement of CFL and NFL games lined up and planned to watch them on the Wardroom's big screen surrounded by pizza, chicken wings and, if he could get it, beer.

This whole thing was a disaster. His ankle throbbed like a demon, school sucked and he'd failed to make the football team. And, there was no way in hell he was going back to Oak Island, even on a tour with other people around. That place was messed up. The whole ghost thing was a mistake – he was washing his hands of it, no matter what the Dean said. Sometimes you had to make the right choices even if no one else agreed.

Sure, the evenings were fun in the Wardroom and ball hockey was turning out to be a blast, but the rest tanked. He'd gotten a C-minus on his first assignment, an assessment he'd felt was charitable given his zero concept of the subject matter. The following week's paper fared worse: a solid D. That was one about Plato and his effing-forms. *See me about revisions*, the instructor had written in bold red pencil. Screw that. The only revision that paper was getting was its crumpled form tossed in the trash. That was the type of *form* Alec understood.

Yes, there were extra sessions offered but no way was Alec doing that. Firstly, he spent enough time in the lecture hall without volunteering more, and secondly, the one time he had shown up, he hadn't understood the material any better than Ashwin's failed attempt to explain it. The concept was too abstract.

He'd give it until Halloween. Another month. If things didn't improve, he was going to quit school and see about getting a job in Fort MacMurray working in the Alberta oil fields. He didn't have any skills, but he'd heard that didn't matter – just show up and be willing to work hard, and they'd find something for you to do. And pay you big bucks doing it.

**

Nora was nervous to stray from campus. After Maggie left, she swept the broken window glass and carefully deposited it in the hall trash can. She

112

debated for a full minute whether it should be recycled or tossed, but decided after weighing all the pros and cons that the trash was safer. Someone might cut themselves if she laid it in the recycling bin.

A couple of girls walked past. "Hey, Nora," they called and Nora smiled back. After her initial reservation, she found her fellow students very friendly. Perhaps Maggie's mannerisms were rubbing off on her, but people no longer ostracized her. University was a world away from high school. Here, everyone was equal and intelligence mattered more than appearance. Nora was guardedly happy. Had she had any idea of how wonderful campus life was, she would have never waited six years to enrol.

She returned to the room, made her bed and then, as an afterthought, straightened Maggie's. She had the idea she might invite Daniel over later, on the pretext they could try to seek Lila Rose together.

When the room was tidy, she checked her appearance in the mirror, added a hint of lip-gloss on a whim, and went off in search of someone in authority to alert them to the broken window.

**

The ghost introduced herself as Myrtle Rogers. "I've been waiting for you," she said amiably to Maggie, who stared at her, immobilized, eyes wide. "I knew you would return." She patted Maggie's hand, or rather, tried to – the motion caused Myrtle's spectral fingers to pass through Maggie's.

"Why?" Maggie asked softly. She was afraid to move – not fearful of the ghost, but worried sudden movement might cause Myrtle to disappear.

"I heard your voice in that dreadful psychic's office. She's a fraud, you know. Madam Denicci could

113

no more summon a soul or predict the future than could that lovely oak tree over yonder."

"But it worked – I mean, *you're* here."

"Only because this is where I live. Or where I used to, before the explosion flattened it. After they rebuilt, I had nowhere else to go. It wasn't always a business, mind you. It used to be a family home, so much nicer when families are around, you know, less lonesome. I so enjoyed looking after my families. There were twelve in all."

Maggie moistened her lips. "That's a lot of families."

"I suppose. Some stayed for a while but most didn't linger... I suppose I frightened them. I didn't mean to, I was just so terribly lonely and longed to be part of a family. I never could bear children, you know."

Maggie stared. It was difficult to gage Myrtle's age. She wore an old fashioned housedress with a faint blue floral pattern, an apron around her middle. The dress came to mid-shin, and Myrtle was on the thin side, but with an ample middle. She had strong, thick hands and Maggie could tell, even from the filminess of them, they were working hands.

"I was thirty-one when my husband killed me," Myrtle said, conversationally. "Everyone assumed I died in the Halifax Explosion. Nobody questioned it, and that murdering bastard got away, scot-free. I've waited almost a hundred years to tell my story." Myrtle fiddled with her dress. "If I'd've known I'd be stuck wearing this dress for all of eternity, I'd have put a little more effort into my appearance. I never liked this old rag to begin with, and let me tell you, dear, after a century of looking at it, I'm about to die from boredom." She chuckled softly. "Ghost humor, dear. Try not to look so worried."

CHAPTER TEN

'...I was born into this life which leads to death – or should I say, this death which leads to life?'
–Augustine's Confessions

"I was a shift worker at the sugar factory," Myrtle stated, settling next to Maggie on the bench. Maggie had to crane her neck to see her, so she shifted her body slowly until she was able to see the apparition without turning her head. At the far end of the park, a mother pushed a stroller, but other than that, the grounds were quiet. "I was so proud of that job. Before the war, jobs were hard to come by for women – it was still frowned upon for females to work outside the home. But with the shortage of men, we were suddenly employable. I worked hard, too – strong arms. My boss used to say that I worked harder than two men put together and was twice as smart. Other than the heaviest of lifting, there wasn't anything I couldn't do.

"My Jimmy came back from the front a changed man. He was injured, you know, sent home with half his right arm blown off. Before the war, Jimmy was the sweetest boy you can imagine, but he came home a shell of a man. He would never speak of what he saw, but it was in his eyes. He was haunted.

"He took to drink. He was angry at the Germans for taking his arm, angry at his former boss for not hiring him back – but he couldn't do the work with only one arm, and Jimmy wasn't educated enough to do anything else. I tried to teach him to read and write but he refused, just got angrier. He started spending time down by the waterfront, drinking homemade hooch with a bunch of bums, wasting their nights trading war stories around a burning barrel."

Maggie closed her eyes, imagining. She could almost see it.

"The day Jimmy killed me started out fine. I'd worked the nightshift, and was exhausted – I'd worked five 12 hour shifts in a row and was so tired I could barely spit straight. When I arrived home that morning, my house was cold. Jimmy had been out all night, hadn't started the stove. I gathered some kindling from the shed and was bent over the stove, trying to get the old bastard lit." Myrtle laughed without rancor. "I had more battles with that stove than you can believe, and that year was the worst. We were late getting wood delivered and it wasn't cured. Plus, Jimmy hadn't covered it properly and it was damp, so it didn't burn well, filled up the kitchen with smoke. It was smoking and I was cursing, and in staggers Jimmy. Drunker than a skunk."

Myrtle began to wring her hands. "I shouldn't have baited him but I was so very tired and cranky myself. It was our wedding anniversary, you see, and I was hoping against hope that he would remember it. Ten years. Why I thought he'd remember it is beyond me. Jimmy was never good at dates, even before the war ruined him." Myrtle sighed, and Maggie thought she could see a hint of tears.

"My boss at the sugar factory was a kind man and he'd seen how hard I was working, was aware of my situation. He knew Jimmy wasn't bringing home any money, and he gave me extra shifts. Just as I was leaving, he slipped me a bonus: an extra five dollars. That was a windfall in those days, let me tell you. I envisioned putting on my Sunday best, going to a fancy restaurant and maybe even the orchestra.

"Jimmy knew payday wasn't until week end, and he came in like a bear, stumbling around, trying to scavenge a few coins to buy more drink. I was more annoyed than afraid, and didn't dare let him know about the five dollars. But Jimmy was after something else – my grandmother's letter opener."

Maggie blinked. "Your what?"

"Oh, I know it sounds ridiculous, dear, to die for something so small. If I had known, I would have given him the letter opener *and* the damn money. Ah, dear, you have the right idea. Don't tie yourself down with any one man. I saw you, you know, with your young man. Handsome he is, too. Although in my day, white women and black men did not mix."

Maggie's mouth went dry. "You saw us?"

"Yes, under that umbrella tree over there." Myrtle pointed and smiled. "Oh, no need to be embarrassed, dear. I must say, you did seem to be enjoying yourself."

"The letter opener?"

"It was Queen Victoria's," Myrtle answered conversationally, as if she was dislodging a juicy bit of gossip. "My great-grandmother was her handmaiden and the Queen gave it to her as a 'thank you' gift. Or, perhaps it was stolen... there were discrepancies in the family lore. Regardless, the letter opener was passed down through generations and my mother gave it to me when I travelled to Canada. It doesn't look like much, mind you – like costume jewelry with paste stones. In the early days, one of my ancestors pried loose the larger jewels and replaced them with imitations, and it was poorly executed, absolutely ruined the whole piece."

"So it wasn't worth anything?" Maggie asked, fascinated. "Why would Jimmy want it?"

"Oh, it's *very* valuable. The larger jewels were removed but the seven smaller ones are intact and they are genuine. To look at it, one would assume it is worthless, but I assure you, the remaining jewels and the silver handle would fetch a bundle. Jimmy came storming in, insisting I hand it over. He'd made a trade, you see – the letter opener for whiskey and gambling debts." Myrtle looked at the ground and sighed. "I had no idea about the gambling, until that point. We got into a terrible row."

"And Jimmy killed you?"

"I'm sure he didn't mean to. I refused to tell him where I'd hidden the letter opener, and he tore the house apart looking for it. He came up from behind me and gave me a mighty shove. I was bent over the stove, still trying to get it lit. It was desperately cold, you could see your breath, and my hands were too icy to work properly.

"When I fell, I struck my head on the corner of the stove and split it open."

Maggie's eyes flew to Myrtle's head. Myrtle saw her looking and obligingly pulled her hair back, showing Maggie the wound. There, indeed, under the mop of hair, was a jagged gash and parts of Myrtle's brains were exposed. Maggie swallowed. "Where was the letter opener?"

Myrtle tried to pat Maggie's hand again, but as before, the fingers drifted through Maggie's flesh. Maggie felt nothing – perhaps a fleeting sensation of cold, but then again, it might have been her imagination. "The letter opener was hidden at my friend's house. I was worried that Jimmy might try to take it – he'd talked about it before. He thought we should sell it, said we needed money more than a useless letter opener. Why, we rarely got mail, so I suppose he was right on that account. But I'd promised my mama I would never part with it, that I would pass it along to future generations. If not my own child, then perhaps a niece. So I left it with my friend and she hid it in her attic. She lived far enough away that her house wasn't destroyed by the explosion, only broken windows."

"And it's been there all those years? In the attic? It's been almost a hundred years."

"No one realized its value, but it was pretty enough not to toss out. I've been keeping tabs on it and the house is being renovated. They are holding a yard sale in two weeks, selling my letter opener for only five dollars. I watched her mark the price myself. Rather ironic, no? Five dollars. If only I had given Jimmy my bonus, I would still be alive. Well, I suppose not – I would have died of natural causes long before now."

"Was Jimmy charged in your murder?"

"No. He knew he killed me, of course, even in his drunken state. He left the house, left me lying on my kitchen floor, my dress hiked up past my thighs, didn't even straighten it out or cover me. The bastard." Myrtle sighed deeply. "Jimmy returned several times, would come into the kitchen and shake his head, then disappear. He looked scared, I'll give him that. I'm not sure if he ever sobered up. The last time I saw him was later that night. He came in, looking something terrible, and left the house with a suitcase. At that time, I was newly dead, and I wasn't sure how to leave my body and follow people yet, so I could only assume he packed up some clothing and fled. That was the last I saw of Jimmy Rogers."

"Surely someone found your body?"

"No, and mores the pity. The neighbors knew I worked nightshifts so they wouldn't come calling during the day. They must have assumed I was working the next night with the house so quiet. They were good neighbors, had an idea that trouble was brewing between Jimmy and me, but in those days, people minded their own business. No one got involved in domestic disputes. Certainly someone might have come by the next day, but the explosion happened in the morning, leveling my house and hiding the secret of my murder."

Maggie's mouth was dry. She'd wanted water earlier, now she was desperate for it, but she remained still. "Everyone assumed you died in the explosion?"

"*Everyone* died in the explosion. Almost everyone we knew. There was no one left to ask questions. It was pandemonium. Mass destruction. No one even suspected."

"And Jimmy?"

Myrtle shrugged. "I suppose he got away. He had a decent start, certainly enough to leave the city, perhaps even the province. He had family in Montreal so perhaps he went there. I saw a lot of ghosts after the explosion, by then I kind of had the whole thing figured out, could move around a bit – I was able to help out. There was as much confusion in the spirit world as the mortal one. So many deaths occurring in the same instant."

"I can't even imagine," Maggie said. "Didn't anyone ever realize that Jimmy was missing? I mean, there was no body, right?"

"After the explosion, the tidal wave hit and that hampered rescue efforts. They might have gotten to my house sooner, but the very next day, a massive blizzard struck Halifax. They say things happen in three, right? Explosion, tidal wave, blizzard. How is that for a triad of Hell? It was *weeks* before they got around to my house. Crews came from all over – all the way from Boston. But the focus was on finding survivors, not burying the dead, not at first."

"But when they finally did clear your house, didn't anyone ever wonder why they only found one body?"

"No dear. You see, there wasn't much left of the bodies to be found. An explosion of that magnitude has a catastrophic effect on the human body." She pointed to her dented skull. "I suppose I should be grateful this is all I have to bear. You should see the explosion victims." Myrtle shuddered. "It's bad – even in the spirit world."

**

The power was still out when the Spirit Seeker Society held their Monday night meeting. The generators kept emergency lighting going and the students walked around with flashlights and candles. Open flames were prohibited because of fire hazard, but everyone ignored the directive. School officials gave up trying to enforce it – the truth was, it was the only way to see when night fell and they were using candle power, too.

The candlelight gave the study room an eerie, romantic glow. No one was sure if the others would show, but they all came on time, with the exception of Alec.

"Should we look for him?" Nora wondered.

"No," Daniel said. "I talked to him earlier. He is very adamant about quitting. What happened at Oak Island?"

"Nothing," Maggie said. "It was a complete waste of time. We didn't even get to the beach."

"Something frightened him," Ashwin added. "Alec refused to talk about it."

"Let's give him time to cool off," Daniel suggested. "Perhaps he'll feel differently by next week's meeting."

"And if he doesn't?" Nora asked sharply.

Daniel shrugged. As always, he was wearing a plain, white v-neck tee and jeans, with tousled hair, and he looked delectable. "Worst case scenario, we don't need him. We can do it with the four of us."

"I've got big news," Maggie said, holding the candle up to her face. It made her look spooky, like her head wasn't attached to her body. "I made contact with my ghost today. Again."

Everyone stared at her in surprise. "Where?" Nora asked. "Here?"

"No, silly, in the Hydrostone. I went for a jog and there she was, in the park. Waiting for me. Her name is Myrtle Rogers. I was hoping to get further proof for you guys, to check census records and see what else I could find out, but with the power outage, there's no Internet."

"So you can't prove it?" Daniel asked.

"Oh," Maggie said, setting down the candle, "I can prove it, alright. Myrtle told me her whole story. She wasn't killed in the Halifax Explosion, she was *murdered*, by her husband, the day before. She told me about a jeweled letter opener belonging to Queen Victoria and told me where to find it."

"Were you scared?" Daniel asked, frowning.

"Sure, at first. But she was sweet. A very amiable sort of ghost. She said she wants to help me. Said I'm in danger. I told her about the Spirit Seeker Society and she said we need to be careful, that we're all in danger." Maggie held up the candle again and looked at each one of them.

"All of us?" Nora squeaked.

"I think so. Before she could elaborate, a man and his dog came into the park and she disappeared. Just poof, there one minute and gone the next. I waited for hours for her to come back, most of the day. But she never did."

Ashwin swallowed heavily. Intellectually, he knew this did not hold up but on an instinctual level, he felt afraid. Goosebumps ran along his arm, up his spine. "This seems like a bad thing," he said, haltingly.

"Are you kidding?" Maggie said. "This is *great!* With the census report and the letter opener, I'll have proof."

"No one will believe you, Maggie," Daniel said. "Even with that stuff, who's to say you didn't make the entire thing up?"

Nora agreed. "He's right. Anyone can access old census records and concoct a story. It's a start, but we need more evidence."

Maggie frowned. This was not the reaction she'd been expecting. "Don't you believe me? Do you think I'm making this up?"

"Of course not," Nora said. "Remember, I saw Myrtle, too."

"What if I bring my camera next time, take a picture?"

"That would help, assuming ghosts can be photographed."

Daniel stood and strode over to the window. Below, the Quad was dark. He scanned the windows in the inner courtyard. "But Maggie has a good point

– we should get proof. Let's each try to find a tangible link to our ghost."

"Like what?" Nora asked. She hadn't even found her ghost. Pier 21 was empty of spirit activity no matter how many times she returned. Nora was starting to think she needed to find better haunting grounds.

Daniel turned to her. Against the dark windows, with the candlelight flickering, he almost looked translucent. As if he was a ghost himself. She could see the lines of stress and worry carved into his handsome face. It came to Nora that Daniel O'Shea had a secret of his own – that he'd been hiding something from them this whole time.

Daniel turned abruptly. "That's it for tonight. We'll meet again next Monday – until then, the Spirit Seeker Society is adjourned."

**

The electricity remained out until Wednesday, and on Thursday, classes resumed. The professors seemed determined to make up for lost time, and students found themselves paying for their three days off with a barrage of assignments. They had finished with Plato and had moved onto Homer, which the students found easier to understand. Alec enjoyed learning about the Trojan wars, Maggie loved the idea of Penelope and her 108 suitors, and Nora found she had a knack for Greek mythology. "The war part is good," Alec stated, "but boy, trying to sort out those Gods are a nightmare."

Daniel offered to tutor Alec, for free. "How do you know all this stuff?" Alec asked him, his frustration evident. "You know as much as the professors. It's like you've taken this stuff before. Don't you find any of it difficult?"

"We covered it in my high school," Daniel said. "I am familiar with most of it, so you're right, it does seem easy for me."

"What high school did you say you went to?" Alec asked.

"You wouldn't know it. Now, look here at these essay statements. You need to choose one. How about 'The Functions of Disguise in 'The Odyssey?''.

"Dude, I don't even know what that means."

Daniel chuckled. "Okay, maybe this will make more sense: 'Explore Father and Son Relationships in 'The Odyssey'.'"

"Yeah. I can manage that," Alec nodded. "I think."

"Don't worry," Daniel said good-naturedly. "I'll help you."

**

The city recovered quickly from the hurricane. Power was restored to most areas, work crews had removed the rubble from the downtown streets, and people returned to work. Still, the gates to the Old Burying Ground remained closed. The damage sustained to the cemetery was not major, but repairing the final resting place of the dead took a backseat to the needs of the living. Ashwin missed the tranquility of the graveyard and took to sitting in the Public Gardens a few streets away. It was Halifax's most treasured communal space – and while extraordinarily beautiful, it did not afford the same sense of peace. Still, he enjoyed people watching and feeding the pigeons and squirrels. The Victorian-style gardens had sustained some damage in the hurricane but trees were trimmed and blooms plucked, and the gates opened up for all to enjoy.

Nora found Ashwin sitting beside a late-blooming shrub rose, its fuchsia colored blossoms resplendent. With the crowd and cacophony of color, Ashwin could almost imagine he was back in Pondicherry.

"What are you doing here?" Nora wondered. She walked through the park regularly and had never before seen Ashwin here.

Ashwin sighed. The feeling of melancholy was threatening to overtake him. His homesickness had increased, bordering on painful. It served to increase his insomnia – at night, his mind would race with thoughts of his homeland, leaving him groggy. He had hoped his studies would keep his mind active, but truth be told, the work was not challenging enough.

Nora took it all in with a glance. "Wait here, I'll be back." She returned ten minutes later with a large chai tea and a container of *gulab jamun* – an Indian dessert. "I don't know if you like this or not, but it was the only thing from the Indian restaurant that was remotely transportable."

Ashwin was overwhelmed. "Nora. That is amazingly kind of you."

She looked away. "Well," she said gruffly, "I figured if we couldn't take you to India, we'd bring India to you."

"Please join me. Sit, please."

She eyed the dessert. "Alright. Let's see if those gulab things taste as odd as they look." She bit into one and her eyes widened in surprise. "My, they are quite tasty. Delicious, actually."

Ashwin smiled. "They are perfect." He took her hand and, for once, Nora did not shy away. "You are a very good friend, Nora Berkowitz. Thank you again."

**

Maggie had returned to the Hydrostone area every day but the ghost of Myrtle Rogers remained elusive.

Most times she'd returned alone, hanging in the park, and even going so far as to pay another visit to Madam Denicci, coughing up another fifty dollars for a Tarot reading and chakra clearing session. It must have worked, her residual negative energy apparently dissipated – this new reading was as benign as it was dull, and the psychic's office remained frustratingly spirit free.

Today, she'd brought Tyrone with her. They'd hooked up a few times since last week's amorous antics, and while fun, it held none of the excitement of that first, randy romp. Worse, they found conversation a struggle. Their fields of study no longer held interest for the other, and when Tyrone went off on a long tangent about enzymoloy, Maggie found her mind wandering to Oak Island and the Money Pit. *What had scared Alec so?* Maybe she'd pushed the limits by climbing into the pit, but still – he shouldn't have quit the Spirit Seeker Society because of it. Maggie felt responsible. It was her fault and she set her mind to resolve it.

"So this is where the ghost was?" Tyrone asked, for the third time.

"Yes," Maggie said impatiently.

Tyrone pointed to the umbrella tree. "You sure? Or is this just a ploy to get some more of Tyrone's sugar-sugar? Come on baby, tell Tyrone the truth." He cupped his crotch suggestively.

Maggie thought of Myrtle saying she'd observed them last time. Ugh. "You know, Tyrone?" she answered. "Maggie doesn't like it when people speak of themselves in the third person."

By the time they caught the bus back to campus, Tyrone understood that he wouldn't be seeing

Maggie anymore, no matter how he referred to himself or how sweet his sugar-sugar.

**

"I'm so frustrated," Maggie said to Nora. It was late, and the girls were in their dorm room. They were attempting to study but both found their minds wandering. Maggie kept thinking about Myrtle, and Nora kept staring at the replaced window pane. From this angle, in the dark, it looked like there was a palm print on it. But when Nora moved, even the slightest, the image disappeared. "I mean," Maggie continued, "how am I supposed to know which yard sale to go to if Myrtle doesn't let me know?"

"Look in the classified ads for yard sales in the Hydrostone area," Nora suggested. *It was definitely a hand print.* And yet, when she moved....

"No, that's just it. Myrtle said her friend lived in a different area, that's why her home wasn't destroyed in the explosion. It could be anywhere."

Nora moved her head back and forth. *Yep. Definitely a hand print. As clear as day.* But why did it disappear when she moved?

"Nora, are you listening? What are you doing? You look like a goose stretching your neck like that."

"Sorry. Does the new window pane look odd to you?"

"No. Why?"

"Nothing. It's just, I see this funny handprint."

Maggie stood abruptly, dressed only in tiny shorts and a skimpy tee, and strode to the window and planted her palm squarely on it. "There, now it's real. C'mon, Nora, I need your help on this."

Nora pulled her eyes away from Maggie's flat, taut belly with the twinkling diamond piercing and looked at the window. Maggie's print dissipated and the ghostly print reformed. Nora shivered and moved her body so she couldn't see it. "Let's figure out what neighborhoods were active in 1917. Far enough not to be affected by the explosion, but not so far that Myrtle couldn't easily visit her friend. She wouldn't have a car, so it couldn't be too distant – close enough to walk or take transit. How did they even get around in 1917? Horse and carriage? I'll check. That should narrow it down, and as it's not really the season for yard sales, there won't be too many listings. We should be able to find it."

Maggie flung herself at Nora and wrapped her arms around her. "That's brilliant." She planted kisses all over Nora's face. "Nora, you're the best."

Nora felt her cheeks grow warm and that funny sensation in her groin again. She was feeling that a lot lately. First with Daniel, then Maggie, even with Ashwin at the park. Her sex hormones were in overdrive. She flushed and pushed Maggie away and surreptitiously glanced at the window pane again.

Yep. There it was. The hand print. Almost like it was waving at her.

CHAPTER ELEVEN

'It is the wine that leads me on,
the wild wine
that sets the wisest man to sing
at the top of his lungs,
laugh like a fool – it drives the
man to dancing... it even
tempts him to blurt out stories
better never told.'
– Homer, The Odyssey

Maggie found out about Nora's birthday by sheer chance. She was snooping in Nora's stuff, looking for coins for the soda machine, when she came across a birthday card from Nora's mother plus a check for twenty-five dollars. It said: *'Happy 25th Birthday to our darling daughter'*. Maggie didn't know what surprised her more: the fact that Nora was twenty-five or that her parents gave her such a small gift. Her own birthdays were extravagant affairs involving expensive electronics, jewelry, and for her sixteenth birthday, a car. Unfortunately, Maggie had crashed it before she turned seventeen, and her father, for once, put his foot down and refused to replace it. No amount of pouting nor tantrums could convince him to change his mind.

Twenty-five dollars. That wasn't even enough for a decent dinner. Geez, a large pizza could set you back twenty-five bucks with delivery and tip.

Maggie thought about what to do. She understood instinctively that Nora would not like a big fuss, but still, a momentous occasion like this could not be ignored. She talked to the male members of the Spirit Seeker Society and they hatched a plan. Nora would not be able to refuse.

"Nora," Maggie said sweetly, "I have a confession to make. I was looking in your dresser for some quarters for the soda machine and I found your birthday card."

"Oh." Nora said.

She didn't look angry, but still, her expression was wary. *But, this was Nora,* Maggie thought, *her expression was always wary.* "So, I was thinking," Maggie began.

"I don't want a fuss, Maggie. Please."

"Let me finish. I was going to say, I know you won't want to make a big deal out of it, but I was wondering if I could take you to dinner? Well, not just you, but everyone. You see, I have a gift certificate for The Five Fishermen Restaurant, enough for all of us to go, and I thought maybe we could have our next Spirit Seeker Society meeting there. It's supposed to be haunted, so it would be perfect."

Nora frowned.

"Please, Nora, think about it. The gift certificate is about to expire. If we don't go, it's money down the drain."

"That place is pretty expensive."

"That's the beauty of it – it won't cost us a cent. Honestly." She could see Nora was wavering. "The ladies washroom is a ghost hotspot."

"Yes, I've heard that."

"Think of it as an academic field trip – for research. It won't be like a birthday celebration at all."

"Okay," Nora said.

"Okay, you'll think about it? Or, okay, you'll go?"

"Okay, I'll go."

Maggie squealed and clapped her hands, jumping up and down. Part one of the birthday present was complete. Now she just had to get Nora to agree to part two.

**

Ashwin rose early, said his prayers, and walked to the Old Burying Ground. Yesterday, there had been a crew there and he was anxious to see the progress they made. Would the gates be open?

Although it was a few minutes before eight on a Saturday, the maintenance crew was already at it. The gates remained locked and Ashwin stood, pondering. At the far side was the old caretaker, minding his own business, his back turned to them. Even from this distance, Ashwin could see him bent over a grave. *What was he doing?* Where the other men had tools – rakes and shovels and chainsaws, it occurred to Ashwin that the old fellow never had anything save his wooden handled hoe.

Ashwin caught the eye of the closest worker. "How long until it reopens?" he asked politely.

"We're almost done – should be open for visitation tomorrow."

"Tell me," Ashwin said, nodding at the old caretaker. "Is he much help?"

The worker frowned. "Who?"

"The old fellow. The regular caretaker. Do you not see him?"

"I don't know what you're talking about, kid."

Ashwin nodded. Yes, it was as he suspected. The hair prickled on the back of his neck. "Thank you," he said pensively, and made his way around the outside the graveyard, keeping close to the wrought iron fence. As he walked, he kept his eyes trained on the old-timer. As Ashwin moved, he matched Ashwin's steps. No matter where Ashwin stood, the old-timer remained at the far opposite.

Ashwin wasn't sure whether to celebrate or to flee screaming. He had found his ghost.

**

Daniel was tutoring Alec in the study room, the same room where the Spirit Seeker Society usually met. Alec wasn't thrilled to awaken early on a Saturday morning – the weekends were his time to catch up on sleep – but Daniel insisted. "It's my only free time."

"Due to football," Alec said flatly.

"Right. Now, let's talk about *forms*. You said you had difficulty with the concept?"

Alec groaned. He thought he'd left Plato's dreaded *forms* behind him forever, but the professor offered to let him redo his paper.

Daniel patted the chair next to him encouragingly. Alec sat reluctantly, arms crossed over his chest. "Close your eyes, Alec, and imagine a chair."

"What?"

"Humor me. Imagine the most beautiful chair in the world. A chair fit for kings."

Alec thought of a throne. Red velvet, encrusted with jewels, carved handles of solid gold.

"Now, imagine sitting in that chair, it's so amazingly comfortable that you never want to leave."

Alec adjusted his vision so the throne became a recliner – the most opulent La-Z-Boy the world had ever seen.

"Now, add heated, vibrating cushions and a built-in cooler filled with beer, right at your elbow."

"Ah," Alec said, smiling.

"Can you envision it?" Daniel asked. "I mean, *really* see it?"

Alec nodded.

"Good. Now, open your eyes and take a look at what you're sitting in."

Alec did, examining the plain, metal chair with the soiled cushion.

"No matter how many chairs you sit in, for the rest of your life, none will be quite as good as your imagined chair, right?"

Alec nodded. He felt the loss.

"Even if you could create it, exactly as you envisioned it, it wouldn't be quite as awesome, right? And even if it was, it wouldn't stay that way. It would get dirty, the cushions would eventually sag, it would show wear from normal use."

"Yeah, I can definitely see spilling beer or crumbs on it."

"So, that's Plato's theory right there." Daniel pointed to the utilitarian chair Alec was sitting in. "When we envision something, it is perfect, and real life can never quite hold up. Everything is just a copy of that original idea. Man, for example, is a copy of God, yet we don't hold up. Even the best men – the smartest, strongest, fastest, most beautiful – are all flawed. They aren't God."

Alec licked his lips and nodded. A light bulb went on. "Holy fuck, I think I finally get it."

Daniel smiled. "Great. Now, let's get started on your essay. Start writing, and let me know when you get stuck."

The finished essay was not bad, but it needed work, and Daniel gently prodded him, suggested alterations, and pointed out spelling and punctuation mistakes. He stopped short of giving Alec the answers, although Alec begged. "Sure, I could write it for you," Daniel said, "but you need to know how to do it yourself. You can do this, Alec. You are smart enough." It took several hours and Alec was exhausted. "I think I pulled a muscle in my brain."

Daniel laughed. "So, now that's done, will you give the Spirit Seeker Society another try?"

Alec frowned. Shivers went down his spine. He felt a cold presence in the room, as if something was watching him. "No. I'm done with that."

"You'll need the mark to pass, though," Daniel said. "Remember, it's worth ten percent of your final grade."

"I don't care." He thought of Oak Island, the terror he'd felt. And he thought of Maggie's ghost, Myrtle. No way did he want to meet up with her, no matter how friendly Maggie said she was.

"What if you just come to the meetings. Just contribute. You don't have to go back to Oak Island. You don't have to find a ghost to be successful at this. Look at me – I'm no closer to finding Lila Rose than when I started. You just have to attend."

It sounded easy. "No," Alec said, gritting his teeth together. He would not be talked into this.

"Just think about it," Daniel said. "We need you, Alec, for this to work."

"What do you mean?"

"You're an important part of the group, Alec. You add common sense to the mix. Sure, Nora and Ashwin are all about the academics, and Maggie brings the 'feel good' quotient to the table, but you are level-headed. We need you."

"Yeah? What do you bring, Daniel? What is your contribution?"

Daniel hesitated. "Besides my charm?"

"Yeah, besides that."

"Well, Alec, it's like this. I am the facilitator. I make it all possible. If someone is having a problem, like yourself," Daniel pointed to Alec's assignment, "then I make sure it gets worked out. Everyone has problems, Alec. Ashwin is terribly homesick and suffers from insomnia. Nora has social anxiety and low self-esteem, and you're refusing to put in the effort academically because you're still clinging to your secret dream of being a professional athlete."

That stung. "What about Maggie?"

"Maggie? Well, Maggie has her own struggle, but it's buried deep."

"There's nothing wrong with Maggie." Alec wasn't sure why he was defending her. "She's perfect."

"Maybe," Daniel said mildly. "But if everything is perfect, why is she so promiscuous?"

Alec gaped. As likeable as Daniel was, Alec didn't care for him. There was something off. It wasn't sour grapes about Daniel winning his position on the football team. Alec had come to terms with that. Mostly. Even had Daniel not made the team, there was no guarantee Alec would have. "Yeah? And how do you propose to fix that? Strap a chastity belt on her?"

"Of course not, this isn't the Dark Ages. Look, Alec, I know you're not my biggest fan, but trust me in this: I'm in it for the long haul. Our little group is very special. I know we're a diverse lot, but the friendships that we forge now will last forever."

**

"Where are you taking me?" Nora asked, eyes narrowing.

"It's the other part of my gift, the best part. Now, Nora, don't be mad – please." Maggie clasped Nora's hands and held them tightly. "Keep an open mind."

Nora looked at her suspiciously. "Tell me this isn't what it looks like."

Maggie bit her lip. "Surprise! I've booked us for a day of pampering. We're getting makeovers."

"No. Absolutely not."

"Please, Nora. It's non-refundable." Maggie screwed up her face tearfully, like she might cry.

"What does it entail?" Nora's voice was even, soft. Maggie wasn't sure how to read it – she expected anger, yelling. Somehow the calm-Nora was more dangerous. She proceeded carefully, knowing she shouldn't oversell it.

"Just the usual," Maggie said, downplaying it. "Mani's and pedi's, facial, waxing, hot-stone massage and haircut. That's all."

Nora's mouth thinned. "Oh, is that all? What's the matter with the way I look?" She caught her refection in the mirror. Her dark hair was a Brillo-Pad-cloud, wiry and wild. She was dressed in black, as usual. *Is that lady a witch?* Could Nora blame that little boy? She *did* look like a witch.

"Nora," Maggie said, playing her trump. "You have a beautiful mind, and every day you nourish it, give it material to make it stronger, better. Please let me do the same for your body. Please let your outside reflect your inner growth."

Nora looked at her reflection again. The witch stared back. "Okay," she said, so quietly the words almost disappeared. Then louder: "But no waxing. I am *not* having my hair ripped out by the roots."

**

Daniel would not be joining them for dinner. His obligation to the football team preempted other commitments. "Mandatory team banquet," he shrugged. "Can't get out of it, sorry."

There was no other time they could all meet. Daniel's only free evenings were Mondays, when the restaurant was closed. Reluctantly, the others agreed to go without him. There was much discussion, but in the end, everyone agreed. With the heavy academic load and everyone's commitments, there was no alternative.

"I'll say 'hello' to the ghost in the bathroom for you," Maggie offered and Daniel laughed.

"You look very nice, Nora," Daniel said, and she looked at the floor, her cheeks flushing alarmingly. "Hey, I should be done by eleven. It'll still officially be your birthday. Shall we meet here for a birthday nightcap?"

"In the study room?" Nora asked, considering. "Well, I still have the beer from the Oak Island trip. I suppose I could sneak it in with a backpack." *Wasn't she being the daring one?*

"Sweet," Alec said, starting to feel better about the evening. He hadn't wanted to come, had needed convincing. "I told you, I'm done with the Spirit Seeker Society," he told them bluntly, not caring how it sounded.

"But surely you're not done with our friendship?" Daniel was the first to speak.

Ashwin was despondent. "Are you, Alec? Are you quitting ball hockey, too?"

"It's just a birthday dinner," Maggie added. "If you don't want to come to the next meeting, we won't force you."

Nora was the clincher. "Look, Alec, if I had to spend my afternoon getting plucked and poked like a free-range chicken, at least you can do is join us. Maggie's treating, you know. Won't cost you a dime."

"And we'll meet back here for beer?" he asked. It actually sounded fun. Lately, it had been harder to get beer in the Wardroom; people were onto his habit of draining their drinks when they weren't looking. "Okay, I'll come for dinner, but that doesn't mean I'm rejoining, got that?"

Maggie clapped her hands. "Oh, we'll see about that. Just wait and see, you'll miss us too much to stay away. We're going to be forever, like the five musketeers."

"Well, four musketeers," Daniel amended.

"Till death do us part," Maggie added.

Alec swallowed, the uncomfortable chill was back. *No way was he going to any more meetings. And, no way was he going back to Oak Island, ever.* Then, he chastised himself for being such a coward. These guys were right – it was just dinner. And they were his friends. Just because he wasn't going to be a member of their society didn't mean they couldn't still hang out.

"Shall we bring you back some cake, Daniel?" Nora asked.

"Oh, don't worry about that – I'll be stuffed from the banquet."

They shuffled out. Nora hesitated. She was disappointed Daniel wasn't coming – there was something between them, she could feel it: almost an electrical charge. Her skin tingled whenever Daniel was near, the fine dark hairs on her arms stood up, tickling her skin. Her breath caught in her throat. There was something about him... more than just his amazing face and body. There was a depth and maturity to Daniel, as if he was an old soul. Daniel made her feel alive. And the way he looked at her 'transformation'; his eyes had widened in surprise and he smiled.

She caught her reflection in the window – and her image stared back at her, ghostly. For once, her hair was smooth. Nora refused to let the stylist cut more than a few inches, but the girl had put in subtle layers which decreased the overall bulk, and plied it with a series of shampoos and conditioners and oils and some sort of straightening balm. Nora hadn't been able to keep it all in order – after getting over the initial discomfort of having a stranger touch her, she relaxed and succumbed to the sensation.

The finished Nora was sleeker and polished. No, she did not look beautiful like Maggie, whose skin glowed and hair bounced with a myriad of shiny blond streaks. But Nora's hair, for once, lay straight and glossy against her shoulders – the stylist had spent a laborious forty minutes with a flatiron. When the unruly locks would spring up again, the stylist sprayed it and ran some kind of shiny lacquer over it. "Whatever you do," Nora was advised, "do *not* get wet."

Nora's finger and toenails were buffed and clipped and decorated with an opalescent purple polish, and she allowed a light makeup application, refusing the heavy base but agreeing to a faint shadowing around her eyes, just a hint of blush. The effect, along with her newly waxed eyebrows, left her looking less stern. Maggie couldn't talk her out of the ever-present black clothing, which Nora wore like a suit of armor, but Ashwin had given her a brightly colored pashmina shawl. "You look like an Indian princess," Ashwin said, wrapping it around her shoulders. Alec looked at his shoes. He hadn't thought to get her anything.

Was she pretty? No, Nora thought. But she felt, for the first time in her life, not ugly, and when she smiled, it was with a confidence that was lacking before.

**

They walked to The Five Fishermen restaurant. It was still temperate although the sun was setting, and the three kilometre walk went fast. As they passed within a few streets of the Old Burying Ground, Ashwin thought about telling the others of his caretaker ghost, but kept quiet. He wasn't quite ready to share that revelation yet. He needed to process it, to come to terms with it. And to get proof.

They had fallen into two groups, Alec and Nora in the lead, with Maggie and Ashwin trailing behind. It seemed an odd pairing, but Alec still felt angry with Maggie about climbing into the Money Pit, and he was able to hold a grudge. He'd grown more comfortable with Nora. In truth, she still scared him, but tonight she was softer and relaxed. Happy. Alec found himself joking with her, surprised to learn that Nora had a decent sense of humor. *Still ugly as sin,* he thought. But this time, when he thought it, he felt a tinge of guilt.

Ashwin found himself telling Maggie about his insomnia, asking for advice. Maggie was their 'health' expert, and was remarkably knowledgeable about natural remedies. "It goes with being vegan," she explained. "With a meatless diet, you need to be careful to keep your nutrients balanced."

"I'm not looking for a radical dietary overhaul," Ashwin said. "I just need something to calm my racing mind at night so I can sleep."

"There are various things you can try," Maggie said. "But really, Ash, sex is the best cure. Nothing like a rousing fuck-session to exhaust you."

Ashwin swallowed. A few weeks ago, he might have thought Maggie was offering her services but now he realized this was just the way she talked. "And the second best cure?"

Maggie laughed and linked her arm through his. "Maybe a nice chamomile tea with a healthy dose of valerian. Leave it to me, Ash, I'll do some research." She looked at him with a teasing glance. "Are you sure you don't want to try cure number one?"

"Quite certain," he answered, primly.

"That's a shame. There's a very pretty Indian girl in my yoga class that I wanted to introduce you to."

"Well," Ashwin said. "Perhaps a combination of both cures might be wise."

**

"Cocktails?" The server asked, and no one batted an eye. The girls ordered cosmopolitans and Alec asked for a beer, and Ashwin motioned to his water glass, requesting a slice of lemon. What he really wanted was coffee – needed the caffeine spark to keep him awake. This lack of sleeping was wearing on him, but Ashwin feared the stimulant would only serve to make sleep even more elusive. Nora ordered a bottle of wine with dinner, and when that went down quickly, she ordered another, and finally, a third. The server didn't blink, just decanted the bottles and awaited Nora's proclamation that the wine "was adequate".

The food was rich and delicious, and everyone declared the salad and mussel bar their favorite. Nora had eaten more mussels than deemed ladylike, and she stifled a belch as the growing tower of empty shells threatened to topple. "All-you-can-eat always seems like a challenge to me," Nora said. "It's good to get your money's worth."

Maggie, having given up her veganism for the occasion, was picking through her own pile of mussels with her fingers, licking them lasciviously, and in her drunken state, Nora found the action erotic. They'd made three trips to the haunted washroom, each time begging the ghost to come out, but the only action they got was disapproving glares from fellow diners.

The server plied them with resident ghost stories and they listened eagerly – and the more they drank, the more they expected to see a ghost. Even Ashwin, who steadfastly stuck to his conviction not to imbibe, found himself looking over his shoulders into the dark corners, waiting for something to appear.

The girls ordered Monte Cristos with their desserts, and by this time Nora was completely drunk. Maggie seemed to be holding it well – "I've had practise," she explained, slurring just a little, which everyone thought was hilarious. Alec had loosened up, had gone back to drinking beer, and was telling Ashwin dirty jokes. Ashwin didn't know whether to be amused or appalled. Maggie didn't eat her dessert, and Nora found herself spooning it into her mouth, although she was fuller than she'd ever been. It would be a sin to let such decadence go to waste.

"Beats the cafeteria food," she said, and again, everyone started laughing.

The bill tallied six hundred dollars.

Nora burped loudly. "That is obscene."

Maggie didn't even glance at it, just laughed and tossed down the gift certificate along with her father's credit card.

"We should take a taxi," Ashwin suggested. "You three are in no shape to walk. It is a good thing we didn't do this on a Monday night after all, I am doubtful you'd make it to classes the next morning."

Alec was telling the server about Plato's *forms.* "It's soooo simple," Alec said. "The *reality* will never match the *ideal.* Mags, give this guy a good tip – buddy's awesome."

Ashwin helped everyone with their jackets and took them outside.

"We should find Myrtle," Maggie said, clapping her hands and bouncing on her toes. "Wouldn't that be fun?"

Ashwin was trying to flag down a taxi, there were several, but none would stop. Finally, a cab pulled up, but the driver took one look at the inebriated state of the trio, and shaking his head, drove on.

"Yes, we *should* find Myrtle," Nora said, jumping up and down like Maggie. It looked so charming when Maggie did it. The road was spinning and she stopped abruptly. "Ugh, I don't feel well." A wave of nausea threatened to erupt. She could taste the mussels regurgitating, mixing unpleasantly with the chocolate dessert and the strong coffee flavor of the Monte Cristo. She burped again, loudly.

Ashwin frowned. "The taxi drivers are worried you'll vomit in their car, and with good reason. We shall have to walk, after all. Are you up to it, Nora?"

"Sure." She put one foot in front of the other and unsteadily began to move. The burping helped so she did it again.

"Ripper," Alec called from across the street. "You burp like a football player, Nora."

Ashwin took Nora's elbow. "Alec, please get down from there, it is unsafe." Alec had straddled the fencing of City Hall, directly across the street in Grand Parade Square, and was attempting to walk it like a tightrope.

"What about Myrtle?" Maggie asked, pouting.

"Oh, my, I have to get you three back home," Ashwin muttered. "Come on, Alec, get down, there's a good lad. Maggie, I don't think it's a good idea to hunt ghosts while you're inebriated."

"Are you suggesting I'm drunk?" Maggie asked, offended. Then she broke down in giggles. "'Cause I am. Shhh, don't tell anyone."

"Drunken ghost hunting is the best time to go ghost hunting," Alec yelled. "It's all about *the forms*. Will an imagined ghost ever live up to the reality?"

"Uh, I think you have that ass-backwards, Alec," Maggie laughed.

Nora bent over and vomited onto the curb.

"Oh, dear," Ashwin said, at a loss.

"Ugh, sorry," Nora wiped her mouth with her sleeve. "I am so embarrassed."

"Don't be," Alec called. "You're supposed to get wasted on your birthday. Right, Mags?"

"We should get wasted with Myrtle," Maggie suggested. "Ew, gross, Nora. Your vomit is purple. Hey, look, it matches your nail polish exactly."

"What? Am I bleeding internally?" Nora moaned.

"No, just the coloration of the red wine." Ashwin looked away. It was causing his own stomach to turn. People were staring. Someone had their phone out; Ashwin had visions of the police coming, arresting them for public disturbance. He would be deported for sure. "Alec," he barked, "Down, now! Take Maggie's hand. That's it. Come now, Nora, we must start walking unless you want to spend the remainder of your birthday in a paddy wagon. Alright." He lined them up. "Everyone hold hands, don't let go."

They stumbled down the street, like a straggle of ducks, Ashwin in the lead. Nora caught her reflection in a store window – her hair was sleek no more. It sprung forth like the unholy hybrid of Ronald McDonald and a yeti.

Alec started to sing and the girls joined in. Loudly and off-key. Nora had vomit splatter on her jacket, speckling her new pashmina shawl, but she didn't seem to notice. Ashwin looked away. He tried to keep to the less busy streets so as not to attract attention, but not so quiet that they'd be a target for derelicts, and he wove them deftly through the streets, like a skilled puppet master.

When they came to the front gates of the Old Burying Ground, he realized they needed to start walking uphill towards the university or they would overshoot it. "This way," he called, leading them to the opposite side of the street.

But Alec broke away, entering the graveyard at a full run. "Maybe Myrtle's in here," he yelled, and Maggie followed automatically.

"Alec, wait up," Ashwin commanded. Nora was bent over again, engaging in a second round of vomiting. By now, all that came out were dry heaves. Maggie had let go of Alec's hand, and was skipping merrily through the front gates. In the far corner, just barely discernible in the gloom, stood the old caretaker. Ashwin swallowed. The old man was staring directly at him, arm held at attention, pointing at them like the harbinger of doom.

"Don't go in there," Ashwin yelled, panic welling up. He tried to slip free of Nora's hand but she held on with a death grip, squeezing his fingers painfully.

"Don't leave me," Nora moaned. "I'm dying."

"Stop," Ashwin hollered, but Maggie and Alec paid him no mind. Maggie was dancing among the gravestones, her hair flying like a Celtic goddess. Alec had climbed onto the tombs, jumping from one to the other, beating his chest like a warrior.

The caretaker slowly swung his outstretched arm from Ashwin and levelled it at Alec.

Ashwin saw it happen in slow motion – could see it unfolding like a theater production but unable to halt it. Alec jumped on a damaged tomb and, inexplicably, rammed it with his shoulder. Although it had stood solid for over two centuries, the marker was unsteady from the hurricane. It gave way as he struck it, toppling onto him, glancing off his skull and crushing his throat. Alec fell forward, silently, no final sound coming from his mouth, tumbling onto the damaged grave below. Nora was looking at the pavement, still heaving, and Maggie continued to dance through the graveyard, blithely unaware.

CHAPTER TWELVE

'No one can see death,
no one can see the face of death,
no one can hear the voice of death,
yet there is savage death that snaps off mankind.'
– Anonymous, The Epic of Gilgamesh

The night Alec Yeats died, Nora dreamt of Lila Rose, hovering over her bed like a dark, beautiful demon. Lila whispered that Daniel killed Alec.

"That's ridiculous," moaned Nora. Her hangover arrived with a vengeance. She vowed never to drink again. Every time she opened her eyes to clear the vision of Lila Rose, the room swirled crazily, and she didn't know which was more frightening: the spectral hallucination or the nauseating dizziness that accompanied the spins.

"He killed Alec." The vision was relentless.

"Daniel wasn't even there," Nora groaned. "Now, g'way."

"He took my life and he'll murder you, too."

Nora came fully awake with a start, her heart pounding so hard it felt like it would rip through her chest. Her eyes were drawn to the handprint on the window, illuminated from the moonlight. It seemed more vibrant tonight.

Her mouth was dry, mealy. She desperately needed water, but the effort involved was too great. She glanced at Maggie, sleeping soundly, limbs akimbo like a starfish and covers thrust off. Maggie was snoring softly, a light, gurgling noise as if she was drowning.

Nora was unable to return to sleep. She lay there as the minutes stretched into hours, as darkness turned to dawn, with heart pounding and throat parched.

**

Alec Yeats' death was ruled accidental. The graveyard was still officially closed due to hurricane damage and no one could explain how the front gates came to be open so late in the evening. A solemn ceremony was held at school, but aside from the other members of the Spirit Seeker Society and a few players from the ball hockey club, Alec hadn't really made friends.

Nora was devastated. "Why did I get drunk? I have *never* been drunk in my life, never even had a drink before, other than a few sips of wine on special occasions. If I had acted more responsibly, this wouldn't have happened."

"It was an accident," Maggie argued.

But Nora knew differently. *She* had been the one to order the wine at dinner. She was the legal adult – Alec was a minor. Ashwin remained silent. Nora felt that he blamed her, too. He didn't say anything, but the reproach was clear in his eyes.

Daniel was the only member who showed up for Monday night's regular meeting. He waited, alone, for several hours, long after it became clear that no one else was coming.

No one seemed interested in seeking spirits at the present time.

The week passed, slipping silently into the next one. The leaves began to change. First there was the odd burst of color, a brilliant red oak or a bright orange sugar-maple. Then, all the trees joined suit, and the city was dressed in her autumn colors. The days were temperate but no longer hot – a definite crispness to the air. At night, it was chilly and the first sheen of frost tinged the Quad in the early morning. People began to replace their lawn furniture with Halloween decorations.

Maggie still wore her sundresses, but she paired them with furry Uggs and a denim jacket, and on the coldest mornings, threw on a pair of leggings. Nora kept with her basic black everything. Daniel never changed – always a white tee and faded jeans, yet he wore them with aplomb, his muscled arms showcasing his summer tan long after it should have faded, a fact Nora drank in often. Even Maggie was caught admiring him with an assessing glance or two. Ashwin took to simplifying his clothing, emulating Daniel. At the encouragement of Maggie, Ashwin traded his dated eyeglasses for contact lenses, and the changes were such an improvement that girls started eyeing him on campus.

It took Ashwin a week to return to the Old Burying Ground. This time, as he entered, he ignored Robert Ross's tomb and walked diagonally across the graveyard, taking care not to step on any graves. Or, he reflected, as few as he could. With twelve thousand corpses stuffed under the ground, there was likely very little area that wasn't directly over a body.

He kept a steady eye on the caretaker. As he got closer, the old fellow became wavery, and Ashwin halted. "I know what you are," he called, clearly. "It is time for us to meet."

He got within twenty feet of the caretaker and the old man simply dissipated. Ashwin halted in frustration. "Coward," he yelled, startling passersby on the street. He lowered his voice, aware he looked like a madman. "Sooner or later, we will talk," he said to the empty air.

He retraced his steps and took up residence on Ross's tomb. He felt very alone. Billi, the little orange tabby, had not appeared since before Alec's death. It was as if the cat recognized Ashwin's anger and stayed away on purpose.

"What does it all mean?"Ashwin sobbed, hugging his knees and letting his back sink against the crypt. "I don't understand what it's all supposed to mean."

**

"I'm going to look for the letter opener," Maggie stated.

Nora frowned. "Are you sure that's wise?"

"Sure, why not? You said so yourself, there won't be too many yard sales this time of year. I've checked the newspaper and there are only five listings. Will you come with me?"

Nora stared at the handprint on the window. Her gaze was riveted to it. Maggie claimed she couldn't see it, no matter how hard she looked, and this amazed Nora. It was right there, clear as day. She'd become fixated on it and stared at it for hours on end. The thought of leaving the small room seemed suddenly appealing. "I guess."

"You will?" Maggie smiled, pleased. But it was muted. Some of the effervescence that was Maggie died with Alec. It was as if someone deflated air from her – she was still Maggie, but she wasn't quite as full, didn't glow. Nora also noticed that Maggie was in their room every night, turning in early, her frequent sexual encounters apparently on hold.

"Should we see if Daniel and Ashwin want to come?" Maggie asked.

Nora thought for a moment. It would be good for the group to get together. To heal. Then, she shook her head. "No."

**

They found the letter opener at the second yard sale. It was stuffed in a box of odds and ends with a five dollar sticker plastered on the outside of the box. At first glance, it was nothing special. But when Maggie held it up to the sky, the sun glinted off the jewels and Nora could see the quality there. "It's heavy," Maggie said.

"Here, let me see." Nora studied it closely. On the handle was a tiny mark bearing proof it was quality silver. The homeowner walked past. "Five dollars for each, or three for ten," she said.

"Excuse me," Nora said, grabbing her arm. "Can you tell us about this letter opener?"

The woman glanced at it. "Not really, it's been in my attic for ages. There were boxes of trinkets when we moved in. Hmm, pretty, isn't it?"

Maggie snatched it from Nora. "Too bad it's in such rough shape. Will you take three for it?"

The woman's eyes flew from the letter opener to Maggie. "Four," she stated shrewdly.

"Deal," Maggie said, slipping the letter opener into her back pocket before the woman could change her mind.

"So, no idea how old it is or where it came from?" Nora persisted.

The woman considered. "No, but it's old. Let's see, we purchased the house from an elderly couple who lived in it for fifty years; they said those boxes of junk were there when *they* bought the house. We've been here for ten, so that puts it back to the 1950's, at least. Say, let me see it again, will you?"

Maggie smiled. Some of her old spark was back. "Sorry, we've love to stay and chat but we can't linger. We've got a very important meeting in the Hydrostone. Come on, Nora, let's not keep Myrtle waiting."

**

Daniel was sitting in the girls' room. He'd taken up residence on Nora's bed and he could clearly see the handprint on the window. Lila Rose was here. He could feel her presence. And he could tell she was very angry.

"Alec died," Daniel said, to the empty room. His face was filled with sorrow. "I was trying to help him. He was struggling, Lila. Not up to the work."

The room remained silent except for the faint beat of music coming from another room and muted chatter in the hall.

"Would Alec have died if I'd gone?" he wondered aloud. "Would my presence have made a difference? Stupid college kids. No more sense than a herd of sheep."

There was a flutter of papers on the dresser, as if a sudden breeze had wafted through the room. Daniel stood and walked to the closed window, sticking his hand over the ghostly print on the pane. He felt Lila Rose's presence. If he breathed deeply enough, he could almost imagine the faint scent of her perfume.

"Please don't blame me, Lila."

**

Billi was back. She was winding her orange body through Ashwin's bent knees, looking for tuna tidbits. "There's no more left, you greedy creature," Ashwin murmured, scratching the feline behind its ears.

The old caretaker had not made an appearance. Ashwin was not fooled; he knew the ghost was there but was choosing not to be seen. He would appear when the time was right. For now, Ashwin had the thin afternoon sun, this funny little cat, and a backpack full of books. On top was the Bible, which seemed a strange book for an Indian boy of Hindu faith, but it was a required text for the Foundation Year. Ashwin felt it was ironic that they were studying the Bible the week following Alec's death. He hoped he might find helpful insight, or at least a channel for grief, but so far it seemed to involve only betrayal and hyperbole.

Another half-dozen books were about ghosts. If Ashwin was to take this spirit quest seriously, he would need to research. Some were novels – the librarian suggested *The Amityville Horror* as the most popular ghost story of all time, and a few were reportedly scientific in nature. One in particular, *The Science of Ghosts*, seemed promising. If he was to become serious about contacting Robert Ross and his ghostly sidekick, Ashwin needed to know what to look for.

**

Nora suggested they take a quick trip to the mall before finding Myrtle. "Let's see if a jeweler can authenticate the letter opener."

Maggie slipped her hand into Nora's. "Great idea. It's pretty crazy that we found the letter opener right where Myrtle said, isn't it?"

Yes. Very crazy. Could it be an elaborate setup? She looked at Maggie, whose face was as open as a prairie field. Nora didn't think Maggie was scheming against her, but still, she had to keep the possibility open.

Maggie was the only one who had seen a ghost. Nora got the sense that Ashwin was holding back, but he stayed mum and it was hard to read his face. Daniel was completely upfront, despite over a month of effort and many visits to their room, he had not made contact with Lila Rose. Had Alec seen something at the Money Pit? Perhaps. He certainly had been frightened enough, but the secret of whatever he saw, or *thought* he saw, died with him. And herself? Yes, she had a brief glimpse of the ghost-Myrtle before she fainted and cracked her head on the floor, but it was only that, a *glimpse*. Most probable explanation was hysteria-induced hallucination. More troubling was that blasted handprint on the window – apparently unseen to anyone else. Nora realized with a feeling of guilt that she hadn't returned to Pier 21 to search for her own ghost in weeks. *I'll go tomorrow.*

The jeweller was fascinated, turning the letter opener over and over, looking at it under a special light and with funny glasses. "The jewels appear to be genuine," he stated. "There are seven in all. Two each of rubies, sapphires and emeralds, plus a single diamond, slightly larger than the rest. The jewels are small but exquisitely cut and of high quality. The silver is substantial, and given the age of it – you believe it belonged to Queen Victoria? If that could be authenticated, it would increase the value enormously."

"But what's it worth?" Nora asked briskly.

The jeweller shrugged. "I couldn't say. You'd need a proper assessment."

"Ballpark it for me," Nora asked. "Just a rough estimate."

The jeweller studied it for a few more moments. "Could be worth thousands, or even a hundred thousand, if you got it to the right auction house. There is a market for this type of collectable, assuming, of course, the authentication holds up."

"Wowsa," said Maggie.

Nora's eyes bugged. A hundred thousand dollars! What she could do with that, or even half, if Maggie would agree to share. It would solve all of her financial problems: pay for her education, even allow for a small car. She would be able to travel home to Truro to see her parents.

"May I ask where you got it?"he inquired politely.

"No," Nora said, her mind still calculating the possibilities, while Maggie answered at the same time: "Four bucks at a yard sale."

He gaped at the girls, looking from one to the other. "I'd say you two ladies have made the find of the decade."

"We had a little help from our spirit friend–" Maggie began, and Nora dragged her out of the store before Maggie could say anything else.

**

"You ain't giving up, are yer?"

Ashwin's eyes flew open. He'd drifted off, the Bible splayed open on his lap. Billi bolted, hissing, running across the graveyard as if the hounds of Hell were on her tail. Ashwin covered his eyes, the low afternoon sun was shining directly into his face and he was forced to squint. Although the old caretaker was standing directly between him and the sun, he didn't block it. It was as if the sunbeam and motes shone through his spectral body.

The caretaker was more ancient than Ashwin imagined. He was a gnarled gnome with a hairless, mottled scalp and dried-apple doll face, all sunken cheeks and hollow eyes. His dress was drab – only slightly darker than his grey skin. His back hunched arthritically and his hands, gripping a wooden handled hoe, were claw-like, with long, ragged fingernails encrusted with dirt.

Ashwin's mouth went dry and he swallowed painfully in an effort to introduce moisture. His heart pounded fearfully, and he was careful to keep his movements slow and small, so as not to alarm his companion.

"Well, whaddyer need to know? I don't got all day, yer know." The voice was thin, querulous.

"You don't?" Ashwin asked.

The old caretaker cackled. "Well now, I reckon I do." He pointed a bony finger at Ashwin. "But while I got the time, I don't got the inclination, if yer get my drift. Why are yer haunting my graveyard?"

Ashwin gestured slowly and deliberately at Major-General's tomb. "Can you tell me anything about Robert Ross? I've been trying to contact him."

The caretaker spit. Or rather, made the action of spitting but nothing came out. "Yer wasting yer time, just like yer wasting mine. That one crossed over right away. Nothing under there but a pile of rottin' bones." The caretaker looked at him shrewdly. "Why're yer interested in him?"

Ashwin sat up straighter. He was fully awake now and his mind sorted through the possibilities frantically. Outwardly, he remained calm. "Ross is a fascinating man, of great historical importance."

"Ah. So that's it." He made the move to spit again and considered. "Never believe what yer read in the history books, boy. They're as much fiction as *that*." He jabbed a gaunt finger at the Bible.

Ashwin swallowed again. He became aware there were others in the graveyard, a group near the front gates and a single viewer walking through the center, reading tombstones. "You killed my friend," he said quietly.

"Pffft. Kid killed himself. Why is it that drunken teenagers feel a need to vandalize graveyards? Has been happening for centuries."

"Are you suggesting Alec killed himself? That's ridiculous. I saw you pointing at him, like the Grim Reaper."

"I was trying to warn yer... could see it happening. He was jumping from headstone to headstone." The caretaker's voice was ripe with disgust.

"I know. I saw him. I should have stopped him."

"There is no reverence. They don't like it, yer know. It angers them to be treated with disrespect. This is a holy sanctuary. They want to rest in peace."

"Yes." Ashwin looked at the ground, remembering. Ashamed.

"The storm disturbed them, true," the caretaker continued, as if Ashwin hadn't spoken. "Loosened the ground, shook everything up. Them markers are old, not steady at the best of times. But after a storm, when the soil is loosened, everything shifts. They don't like it."

"What are you suggesting?" Ashwin asked, his voice a raspy whisper. "Are you suggesting *the dead* had something to do with Alec's death?"

"I ain't saying nothing. Now, what do yer want to know about Robert Ross? I'll tell yer what I can, and then you need to bugger off. Stop bothering me. I've work to do."

CHAPTER THIRTEEN

'Hell is empty and all the devils are here'
–William Shakespeare

The weather turned cold during the third week of October. The stone walls of King's did not retain the heat, and the students found themselves piling on extra sweaters. The underused pathways, which connected the residences to Prince Hall, found a sudden popularity. No one wanted to venture into the frigid courtyard, especially the residence students, who were prone to wandering the halls in their pajama bottoms and flip-flops.

The football team continued their weekly games, winning enough that they'd secured a berth in next weekend's semi-finals. Depending on the outcome of another team's game, the match might be held at Wickwire Field and the players were praying for home advantage.

Ashwin continued playing ball hockey, without Alec, and at his invitation, Maggie joined the team. She was naturally athletic and added value. Maggie was, Ashwin reflected, the quintessential Canadian girl: pretty, popular and vivacious. Ashwin realized he had grossly underestimated her. She'd come through in her promise to find him a sleep remedy, not forgetting even in the wake of Alec's tragic death. While the valerian-laced chamomile tea had not yet achieved its desired effect, it wasn't for lack of effort on Maggie's part. She was also surprisingly intelligent. He'd proofread her theses, and while not as literate as Ashwin's own, Maggie's offered a freshness and originality that delighted the professors. She averaged a solid A minus, never receiving less than a B.

Nora was stuck at B minus. Her study ethic was second to none and her research impeccable, but she was unable to think outside the box – struggling with the independent ideas that would lift her papers to excellence.

Daniel had no problem with the work. He never showed his papers to his peers, but it was clear from the ease at which he discussed the topics that he knew the subjects inside and out. The Spirit Seeker Society seemed to spend as much time discussing academics as they did ghosts, especially during this season of midterms, and their work improved because of it. They had left behind the Ancient World and were immersed in The Middle Ages – and Monday night meetings were spent dissecting *Dante's Divine Comedy* or *Augustine's Confession*. The death of Alec Yeats drew them together and gave them a new platform, and the quartet delved into the concepts of immortality, of sin, of eternal love. They did not speak of Alec, nor the Oak Island venture and, certainly, never of Nora's ill-fated birthday, but they carried his memory with them. Each member felt his presence.

The proof of the jewelled letter opener was the catalyst for propelling their spirit search. Daniel was especially fascinated with it, and he asked Nora or Maggie to hold it up to the light, never asking to touch it himself.

"It's like he's afraid of it," Maggie said. "Notice how he's always careful to keep his distance?"

"What I don't understand is how he isn't *frozen*," Nora added. "Look at the rest of us, bundled up like it's the Ice Age, and it hasn't even gone below zero yet. Poor Ashwin looks like he's in pain – I don't think he's ever experienced a cold climate before."

"How will Ash survive January or February?" Maggie wondered.

Nora purchased a portable heater at the thrift store and plugged it into an outlet in the study room. Ashwin settled his chair in front of it and smiled gratefully.

"Daniel must be one of those naturally hot-blooded people, you know, the type who never feels the cold." Nora fantasized about the touch of his skin – would it be hot? She had no idea. As with the letter opener, Daniel was careful to maintain his distance. As their friendship grew, Nora made a tentative move to touch his hand or arm, but he always moved deftly and subtly out of reach. Yet, he seemed to enjoy her company. Was he attracted to her? Nora scoffed at herself. *How could he be?* Even after her makeover, Nora knew she was on the wrong side of ugly. *How could anyone who looks like Daniel be attracted to someone who looks like me?*

Yet he vied away from Maggie as well, a fact that didn't go unnoticed by the bubbly blond. "Maybe he's gay? Or a germaphobe?" Maggie hypothesised, and Nora was pacified. It helped that Daniel wasn't all over Maggie, like every other male on campus.

After a brief hiatus, Maggie had resumed her sexual prowess, racking up two or three lovers per week by Nora's estimation. It was as if she was making up for lost time. Maggie rarely saw the same guy twice, much to their chagrin. There was a wake of broken hearts trailing behind Maggie, but she seemed oblivious. Nora and Maggie had come to an agreement – after Nora had walked in on her in *flagrante delicto* – twice, they devised a system.

Maggie could entertain *guests* during the weekends, but not during school nights. Nora was adamant. The B minus stung; she needed her study time to raise her average and there was no way she could concentrate with some random male's bare-ass boinking in the next bed.

They had not been able to raise Myrtle again. No matter how many times they returned to the park near the Hydrostone, either alone or in tandem, the Spirit did not appear. Maggie suggested seeing Madam Denicci again, and while their visit was much more pleasant than their initial reading, the psychic's domicile remained Myrtle-free.

Nora had no more luck with her own spirit quest. She'd returned to Pier 21 three times, spending hours poking through the exhibits, talking to the curator, trying to keep an open mind. She'd found out that the old fellow manning the entrance liked his coffee with two sugars and two creams, so she began bringing him a *double-double*, and sometimes threw in an apple fritter to sweeten the deal. The way to any Maritimer's heart was via Tim Horton's, and Nora took full advantage of the coffee culture.

She'd learned his name was Tom, that he was a widower and excruciatingly lonely, and Nora felt ashamed for her earlier assessment of his perversity.

Eventually, Nora confided in Tom, told him about the Spirit Seeker Society, and he became a champion of her cause. No, he hadn't seen any ghosts at Pier 21, but that didn't mean they weren't there. "The key," Tom enthused, "is to find someone who died of trauma or heartbreak. Perhaps shortly after they arrived." There were a great many ill people who travelled the seas in those days. Ocean travel was perilous, and the squalid conditions of many vessels proved a recipe for death. Often, travellers were not in good health to begin with, and the journey took weeks, if not months.

There was also no progress on the Lila Rose front. Even though the handprint remained on the window, unseen by all but Nora, Lila remained hidden. Yet, sometimes things fluttered in the room for no reason. Items were rearranged. Who could tell with Maggie's belongings, which continued to be strewn far and wide, despite Nora's best intentions, but Nora was meticulous with her own things and she could tell when stuff had been tampered with. Maggie swore she hadn't touched it and Nora wasn't sure what to believe.

The jeweled letter opener was the item most likely to be moved. Maggie liked to leave it on her desk, in full view, despite Nora's admonishments that it might be stolen, especially given its value. "People don't steal things here," Maggie said.

"Yeah, right," Nora answered. "What about my duffel bag? You put it out for a few minutes while I was sweeping and someone grabbed it right off."

"That's different," Maggie said. "If it's out in the hall, it's considered fair game."

"So why did you put it there?"

"Well, I didn't think anyone would take *that*. Let's face it, Nora, it was butt-ugly and the clasp was broken. It was no better than trash."

The assessment stung. Yes, it had been of poor quality, but it was the only suitcase she owned.

The letter opener became a game of sorts. Maggie would place it somewhere and when they came back from classes, it was moved. Not always, but sometimes. It didn't matter where she put it – it was rearranged. The other item that seemed to be played with was Nora's birthday check. She never cashed it. Wouldn't. Twenty-five dollars might seem like a paltry amount to Maggie, but to Nora's parents, it was substantial and she knew they could ill afford it. This time, the thought counted more than the gift, and Nora kept it pinned to her bulletin board. She found it comforting, like a totem of her parents affection.

Yet, occasionally she would find it sitting on the window pane, underneath the handprint. Or, on her pillow. No matter how securely she tacked it, the check moved, with the tack remaining firmly on the board. There was a message here, but the girls were at a loss to decipher it.

Nora delicately broached the subject of selling the letter opener. Again.

"No." Maggie was adamant.

"Look, Maggie," Nora said. "You come from a wealthy family – money means nothing to you. But for me, it would make a world of difference. I can't even afford a cup of coffee half the time."

Maggie wouldn't budge. "I promised Myrtle I'd take care of it. Not sell it."

"Just think about it, Maggie. Please."

Maggie was firm, and Nora saw the steely core under her fluffy, affable layers. "I'm not selling it, Nora. And that's final, so stop bugging me about it."

**

Nora brought Tom his *double-double* and his face lit up. "Hey," he said, after taking his first swallow of coffee, "I made some inquiries for you. Talked to my sister Linda, remember I told you about her? She was the one who went to school with Lila Rose. They weren't friends, but they lived on the same floor. Linda's room was a couple of doors down."

"Oh?"

"Seems Lila Rose had a suitor. Linda thinks he had something to do with her death."

Nora frowned. She had helped Daniel do research – he'd asked her to gather data at the library while she was there and she'd skimmed the material, seeing if fresh eyes would pick up something. It seemed the least she could do since her own spirit-search was barren. "The reports never said anything about a boyfriend."

"He was an *unwanted* suitor. Linda said he pestered Lila all the time, and that he became belligerent when she wouldn't return his affections."

"But the police reports stated the room was locked from the inside."

"Therein lies the mystery," Tom agreed. "But think about it. Unrequited love is a definite motive."

Nora considered. "Do you know his name, Tom?"

"Sure. Alan Dressier."

Good. It would give Nora an excuse to find Daniel, to give him a lead.

**

The day was overcast and raw. Very few leaves remained on the trees, and the city had taken on a different look. Ashwin had bundled several sweaters under his jacket, but still he felt chilled. He could not imagine what it would feel like when it officially became winter.

Was he the only one who felt the cold? Some people were still wearing *shorts!* How peculiar. Did they really not mind the falling temperature, or was it an idiosyncrasy of Canadian behavior? Were they trying to prove how tough they were, or perhaps trying to stretch out summer as long as they could before the first snowfall? Daniel certainly seemed impervious to the cold – he still wore the same short sleeved tee-shirt as he had when they first met. Ashwin couldn't fathom it, and he thought longingly of Pondicherry, where the temperature rarely dipped below twenty degrees Celsius.

He was determined to get answers today, before the weather grew too cold. He was armed with a blanket for his knees, a mug of Chai tea, and a container of tuna for Billi. The little cat arrived presently, and he stroked her back as she greedily lapped up the fish.

The caretaker-spirit was absent.

He closed his eyes and thought about Major-General Ross, tried to envision the soldier as if he stood before Ashwin in all his British finery.

Had he dozed? Ashwin couldn't be sure, but it certainly seemed a dream as the caretaker appeared before him, laying one grey, withered hand on Ashwin's. Everything faded, except for the indignant hissing of Billi as she clawed herself across Ashwin's lap in a frantic effort to flee.

And suddenly Ashwin was there, standing on a little bluff, overlooking the battlefield. The Spirit stood beside him, and Ashwin saw he was a much younger version of himself. No older than Ashwin, and he wore the woolen tunic of a foot soldier.

It was hellishly hot, the kind of humidity Ashwin was familiar with in India. Ashwin could feel the beads of perspiration drench his body, could feel the scratchy fabric as if he was wearing a uniform instead of his own clothing. "'Twas the stench that got you," the caretaker said. Although the battlefield was in the distance, the pungent odors assailed them as if they were standing knee deep in it. It reeked of acrid smoke from the gunpowder, which burned his eyes, nose and throat. Of vomit, and urine and feces – body fluids released en masse from the injured and dying. The faint smell of whiskey as soldiers poured it into open wounds or tipped the canteens in their own mouth. "Their canteens are filled with alcohol instead of water," Ashwin whispered, entranced.

"Aye, or poppy tea."

Ashwin looked at him quizzically and the caretaker elaborated. "Twas the soldier's best friend, something a soldier could brew himself. It was more available and effective than whiskey for pain. And, if they were uninjured during the battle, a few sips of poppy tea would help them sleep afterwards."

"Yes," Ashwin nodded. "I've heard of it under a different name, we call it *doda*. It is very popular in Asian and Indian culture."

The caretaker began to move forward, and Ashwin followed, carefully stepping over the injured and dead. *Could they see him?* Ashwin didn't think so, but as one dying man, moaning and crying and hollering, begging for help, looked up, he seemed to stare Ashwin directly in the eye.

"We call that the *Holy Trinity of the Battlefield*," the caretaker said, nodding at the man. "The dying always beg for the same thing: water, mother and God."

Some screamed for all three. "Why won't anyone help them?" Ashwin asked, shaken.

The caretaker shrugged. "Who's around to help 'em? Most will die from their wounds long before aid arrives. The rest will die from infection."

"But that's... barbarous."

The Spirit ignored him, pointing a skeletal finger ahead, and Ashwin followed his outstretched hand, seeing Robert Ross. The general had halted his ebony steed and was apparently conferring with his men. He wore the British redcoat with a gold braid adorning one shoulder. For a moment, he removed his black-plumed hat and wiped his brow.

"He's smaller than I expected," Ashwin said. "But just as regal. Where are we?"

"North Point."

"Outside Baltimore? This is it, the day Ross dies?"

The caretaker didn't deign to answer, just held his arm aloft and pointed, and the scene changed abruptly. They were outside a farmhouse, and Ross was ordering the farmer to make breakfast for himself and his staff. His tone was cocky, self-assured. "And be quick about it, man. We have a battle to fight."

The farmer was furious. Ashwin could see his eyes flash anger over his fear, making him foolhardy. "What makes you think I'd waste my eggs and pork on British dogs? You, sire, are mine enemy."

Ross laughed. "Feed us now or I'll burn your farm and slaughter your animals. We arrive from setting Washington ablaze and your squalid farm is nothing but a bump in the road. We have no quarrel with the American peoples. We will spare your property if you cooperate."

The farmer spat. "You are nothing but common criminals."

"Nay, Sir, 'tis the American government that is unlawful. Our actions are in answer to the burning of York – we are the respondents, not the aggressors." Ross signalled to a soldier who held aloft a torch. "Will you prepare food for mine self and staff, or will I set your land ablaze?"

The farmer capitulated and Ross dislodged from his horse, a striking black stallion. A scuffle ensued on the far side of the barn, and Ross halted mid-step as his soldiers brought forth three American prisoners. They were bedraggled – their uniforms not nearly as fine as the British.

"Splendid," Ross said, observing the captured cavalrymen. "Tell me, what awaits us in Baltimore?"

"Twenty thousand soldiers and two hundred cannons," the prisoner hissed angrily. "You will *not* take Baltimore."

Ross smiled, removing his gloves and wiping his sweating brow. "I should think, Sir, if they are the same quality of militia as met us in Washington, we shall dispense of them quickly."

The vision blurred and sped ahead. The men had finished dining and were preparing to leave. The prisoners had been removed, and the farmer stood alone, wringing his hands. As promised, Ross had left his buildings untouched. The farmer couldn't refuse one last dig. "Will you be returning for supper?"

"Nay," Ross responded, seemingly in high spirits. "I'll sup tonight in Baltimore – or Hell."

Ashwin turned to the caretaker. "Ross doesn't suspect the Americans are waiting only a few kilometres down the road." He had studied the history – he knew what came next.

"Yes. The Americans were appalled at his arrogance. Imagine, stopping the forward march to appease his belly. Still, I suppose he may have tired of the poor quality camp food. 'Twasn't much finer for the officers as for the troops, just daily rations of weevil-infested bread, and beef so foul it needed boiling to be edible."

"I've seen enough," Ashwin said, turning away. "Take me back."

"Nay, yer'll see it to the end."

The scene changed. They were riding through a wooded area now, and the sound of musket fire sounded from ahead. Ross spurred his horse forward. He would advance to the front to fight side-by-side with his men. Patches of fighting were everywhere. Ashwin could see men from both sides falling to musket balls. Then a volley of activity and Ross was down, tumbling from his horse. Two snipers lay hidden in the trees, and they were flushed out and executed with an expediency that Ashwin found alarming.

"I do not need to see this," Ashwin was repelled and turned away. The casual manner of death left him feeling queasy. Blood poured copiously from Ross's neck, but the man was lucid, speaking of his wife, of his country.

The caretaker looked at Ashwin harshly. "Major-General Robert Ross made the poor decision to stop for food, didn't he? He allowed his enemy to prepare, to ambush him. His choices led to his downfall, as will yers, Ashwin Pawar."

"I have not made poor choices," Ashwin said, quietly, but in his heart he knew that was untrue. Yes, he had chosen not to partake of the drunkenness that contributed to his friend's death, but perhaps that very decision was the deciding factor. Had he been drunk like the others, he would not have led them along the streets – they would have taken a different route, and Alec spared his deadly tombstone jump.

Ashwin spent his life on the sidelines, observing instead of doing. Even now, on the greatest adventure of his life, when he should be embracing the excitement of a new country, he remained a bystander. He did not seek the adventure of exploring the treasure of Oak Island, preferring to sit passively aside. Yes, he rationalised, he was on a student visa and could not afford trouble, but his heart ached for adventure, not for hearing about it. He spent his days in a graveyard, full of death, instead of embracing life.

He had not the courage to stand up to his father, even regarding something as important as his education. He wished to stay in India, to attend one of the many fine universities there, not be shuttled halfway around the world like an embarrassment.

Robert Ross had lived his life valiantly, and how had it ended? Slaughtered in a foreign wood, forever unreturned to his loved ones and the country he fought and died for. Instead, Robert Ross's body was stuffed ingloriously inside a barrel of rum, shuffled from ship to ship until he was offloaded in Halifax and placed in an overcrowded, public burial ground.

"*I've seen enough,*" Ashwin barked. "Return me to present day, *now.*"

When the vision cleared and he found himself, alone, in the cold graveyard, Ashwin hastily gathered his belongings and walked quickly from the Old Burying Ground, vowing never to return.

Had he really seen this or was it a hallucination, brought on by his sleep deprivation? Perhaps he was going about treating his insomnia in the wrong manner. Instead of lying passively, praying for sleep while his mind raced, perhaps he needed to increase the potency of his innocuous herbal beverage.

An idea popped into his head as he passed a Chinese emporium, just a ratty little shop tucked between a pizza joint and a used book store. He'd walked this way many times but had never noticed it. Ashwin stepped through the door, immediately feeling the warmth of the shop and the cloying aroma of incense. The elderly proprietor looked up.

"Do you carry doda or poppy tea?" Ashwin asked.

CHAPTER FOURTEEN

'Be still my heart; thou hast known worst than this'
–Homer

The four surviving members of the Spirit Seeker Society gathered in Nora and Maggie's room on Halloween night, the anniversary of Lila Rose's murder. "If ever there was a night to materialize, this will be it," Maggie reasoned. "No costume, Daniel?"

Daniel looked at his jeans and white tee and smiled ruefully. "Didn't think I could carry off the sexy cat routine."

"More like slutty cat," Nora murmured. She had a nagging headache that had been plaguing her for days and her throat was sore, the sure signs of an impending cold. She was feeling particularly cranky. But even through her foul mood, Nora had to admit that Maggie looked adorable. And *very* sexy with her sheer black leggings and thigh-high leather boots. *How was she able to navigate in those things?* The stiletto heels were at least six inches high. Nora's feet cramped just looking at them. Nora looked down at her own costume: a witch. *Why not? Might as well work with what you've been given.*

Ashwin was dressed as a pirate. In preparation, he hadn't shaved for the past few days and his dark stubble, along with some kohl lining around his eyes, gave him an authentic Barbary Coast vibe. "As a child, I'd hear stories of dressing in costume and begging for candy," he said wistfully. "It sounded jolly. I was ever so envious."

"I'll go with you to a few houses," Maggie offered, "so you can have the full experience."

"They're likely to slam the door in your face," Nora said. "Trick-or-treating is for children."

"Oh, loosen up, you old witch," Maggie said, and everyone chuckled.

To facilitate the process, Maggie brought an Ouija Board, Tarot cards, and plenty of candles, even though open flames were expressly forbidden in dorm rooms. "We need to set the mood," she rationalized.

"Why Tarot cards?" Daniel asked. "Do you know how to read them?"

"Well, no, but I wanted to provide a channel for Lila Rose to speak to us – especially as she seems so reluctant."

"But," Nora said, "if you don't know how to read them, how will you know what she's saying?"

"I'll wing it. Plus, I brought this," she pointed to a dog-eared copy of *'Tarot For Dummies'*. "In case we need translation."

"Clever," Daniel said, admiringly, and Nora bristled. He was right: it *was* smart of Maggie to prepare but still it irked to hear him say it. Nora moved her body between Daniel and Maggie, so he could no longer see Sexy Cat's sexy-ass from where he was sitting.

"I take it the Ouija board is for the same purpose?"

"Exactly," Maggie beamed.

Nora shifted. "I'm not really comfortable with the Ouija board, Maggie. Isn't it a tool of the Devil?"

"Well, sure, in the wrong hands," Maggie said. She looked at the three of them and laughed. "Relax, you guys, it was just a joke. It's a game, but it might give Lila Rose a vehicle to communicate." She lit the candles. "Now, let's get cracking. I've got oodles of Halloween parties lined up."

Ashwin produced a thermos and cleared his throat. "I have something to share. Poppy tea."

Everyone gaped.

"It is a natural Asian herbal brew used for centuries to increase energy and foster a sense of well being. I thought if we were relaxed, it might help open our mind to the possibilities."

"Awesome," Maggie said. "Pass it over."

"Are you insane?" Nora asked. "It's a drug."

"No," Ashwin explained patiently. "It is completely organic. I brewed it myself from poppy seeds. Although, it does have mild analgesic qualities. Do you still have your headache, Nora? It may help alleviate your tension."

"I'm not tense," Nora said acridly. "I'm completely relaxed." A tiny vein pulsed in her forehead.

"Ashwin's right," Maggie said. "Poppy seeds are completely safe, they aren't the part of the plant that opium comes from. I mean, they're used in baking, for heaven's sake. People give them to toddlers. For instance, poppy seed muffins. You eat them all the time."

Daniel peered into the thermos, careful not to touch anyone in the small space. "This seems unlike you, Ashwin, to do something so..."

"Free spirited?" Ashwin asked. "Adventurous? Well, get used to it: this is the new me. I, Ashwin Pawar, will no longer be a passive observer in my own life."

"Smells... interesting," Daniel said, sniffing. "But I'll have to pass. Poppy seed allergy. I'll swell up like a balloon and break out in hives."

"Allergy-Guy," Maggie said, snapping her fingers. "Think we found your Halloween costume." She batted her eyelashes, just a little.

Daniel laughed. "If you were dressed as a nurse, I might give it a try. But as Sexy Cat, you'll be no help at all."

Were they flirting? "We're getting off track," Nora said sternly. Her head pounded and she rubbed her forehead to release the tension. She'd taken some Tylenol before but it wasn't helping. "Ugh. Your tea smells like ass."

Ashwin frowned. "It does, a little. I followed the recipe and added lemon juice. Perhaps I should have added more." He poured a little into a paper cup and passed it to Nora.

"Drinking flavored beverages from Dixie cups. How can this scenario possibly turn bad?" Nora's voice dripped with contempt.

Maggie pushed past her and took the cup, her cat-tail brushing against Nora. She sipped tentatively, then downed it one gulp. "Not too bad once you get past the initial taste. How long does it take to work, Ashwin?"

"The effects should be immediate, I believe." He followed Maggie's example and drank his cup quickly. He felt empowered. The new Ashwin was fearless.

Nora caught Daniel's eye and he shrugged good-naturedly. Should she try it? *No!* The word sounded strong and clear, as if it had been whispered directly into her eardrum. Nora's eyes flew to the handprint on the window. It almost glowed.

"Lila," she said, the words coming out in a croak. "Lila Rose is here."

Maggie flew into action. She had the Ouija board out of its box and set it on the bed, then splayed out the Tarot cards, face down. "Talk to us, Lila," she said. She put her hands over the Ouija board and hovered.

Nothing happened.

The minutes stretched.

Daniel shifted slightly and the movement seemed to unglue everyone. Ashwin randomly turned over a couple of Tarot cards. One was the Three of Swords which Nora recognized from Madam Denicci's reading. She couldn't remember the meaning, though. The other was of a smug-looking fat man in a purple tunic, surrounded by nine golden cups.

"It's moving," Maggie said, suddenly. "Somebody write this down. The first letter is M."

Nora scrambled for a notepad on the desk.

Maggie called out the other letters and Nora tracked them in her tiny, neat penmanship. "M. U. R. D. E. R."

Nora rolled her eyes. "Stop goofing around, Maggie. That's not funny."

Maggie grinned. "C'mon, admit it, it's a little funny."

"You certainly had me going," Ashwin said, expelling his breath.

Daniel frowned. "I have to agree with Nora, Maggie. That was in poor taste."

"Oh, lighten up. It's Halloween. Where's your sense of trickery?" Maggie wiggled her fingers in the air and said, spookily, "This is a night for the macabre." She turned back to the Ouija board. "Who killed you, Lila Rose? Speak now or forever be doomed to the pits of Hell, for all of eternity."

Nora panicked. She could feel fingers squeezing her throat but when she put her hands up, nothing was there. "Stop it, Maggie!"

The planchette toggled across the Ouija board of its own violation.

"Look!" Maggie said, her eyes growing wide. "It's really working. I'm not doing anything this time, I swear. Maybe she's trying to say she really was murdered. Who killed you, Lila Rose?"

The candles blew out and the room was plunged in darkness. The only light came through the window, from the courtyard lamps of the Quad. Nora scrambled to turn on the overhead lights but, as before, nothing happened.

"Is this really happening?" Ashwin asked. "Or is the poppy tea giving me hallucinations?"

"No, this is real," Maggie said, her voice excited. "I feel nothing from the tea."

"Nothing?"

She shook her head. "You?"

Ashwin shook his head, feeling disappointment. The one time in his life he had the courage to play outside the boundaries and it was a failure. "Perhaps I should have brewed it stronger."

They drifted off in silence. Maggie kept her hands hovering over the Ouija board. Ashwin concentrated on the Tarot cards, but none seemed to beckon him as before. The constriction around Nora's throat had eased the moment the candles blew out. Nora moved her hands up to her temples and rubbed without thinking. Her headache was intensifying. Daniel stayed so still that Nora could not even see his chest rise and fall in the darkened room. Finally he let out a long sigh. "She's gone," Daniel said. "Nora, try the overhead light again."

Nora complied and this time the light clicked on. They all looked at each other.

"What did that mean?" Ashwin said. His eyes were round – appearing even wider from the kohl liner.

"It means we're getting close," Maggie said. "Lila Rose is finally starting to communicate."

Daniel looked nonplussed. "You may be right, Maggie. It's clear she's gone, for now. Well, fellow members of the Spirit Seeker Society, I believe the show is over for tonight."

**

Maggie took Ashwin trick-or-treating to a half-dozen houses adjacent to campus, and only one of the occupants made a snippy comment questioning if they weren't a little too old for this. "He's from India," Maggie said. "He wanted to have the full Halloween experience."

"From Pondicherry," Ashwin added helpfully. This was marvellous. He could do it all night.

"Still nothing from the poppy tea?" he asked Maggie as they navigated the path to the next house.

"Nope, nothing more than a normal cup of Earl Grey. I think you're right, maybe it wasn't strong enough or the seeds were stale. You've got to be careful, though, other countries don't have the same regulations as we do – they use harmful pesticides. They can be filled with all sorts of contaminates."

"I purchased them locally."

"They should be fine, then. It's when you order straight from China on eBay it can be dodgy. Hey, I've got some off-campus parties lined up, want to join me?"

"Thank you, but no. I signed up for the karaoke competition in the Wardroom."

"I didn't know you could sing."

"I can't. Certainly not well."

She laughed. "Wow, Ashwin, I'm impressed. Seems like you've really come out of your shell."

He thought of Major-General Robert Ross and the horror of the battlefield, the fleeting nature of human life. He had not told anyone about his experience. "Let's just say, I had an epiphany of sorts."

**

Daniel watched Nora tidy the room. "Aren't you going out?" he asked, pointing at her costume.

"No," Nora said, removing her witch hat. "I planned to, but I'm feeling a little off. I'm coming down with a cold – think I'll just turn in early, maybe get a jump on next week's reading."

"Perhaps you should have tried the poppy tea after all," he said.

"No thanks," she grimaced, remembering the foul odor. "I'd probably end up with a wicked case of diarrhea." *Oh, great, Nora: talk about poop, why don't you? Just what every guy wants to hear... very attractive.* She decided to deflect the attention. "I can't believe Ashwin brought it – Maggie, yes, but Ashwin? So out of character."

"Ashwin is becoming North Americanized."

"Yes," her mouth thinned. "And I suspect that's not a good thing. Oh, Daniel, I almost forgot: I learned that Lila Rose had a stalker. A guy named Alan Dressier. Did that come up in your research?"

Daniel's eyes widened momentarily. "Where did you learn that?"

"I've been spending a lot of time at Pier 21, trying to find my own ghost. Big waste of time – but I've gotten to know the ticket guy. His sister went to school here. He knew all about Lila Rose."

181

Daniel drummed his fingers on the table, considering. "Hmm. I'll check into it. Well, Nora, if you don't need me for anything else, I'd better go."

"Sure." She held the door open for him and watched him leave. *Why did she feel so disappointed? What did she think would happen? That Daniel would tear off her ugly witch costume and make passionate love to her on her narrow dorm room bed?*

No, of course not, Nora chided herself. But he could have stayed and chatted for a bit. Didn't have to leave as if his pants were on fire.

**

Maggie stumbled back to their room in the middle of the night, a drunk and sobbing mess. "Oh, Nora," she cried, throwing herself onto Nora's bed. "Everyone was so mean! Especially the girls."

Nora was groggy. Her throat was worse and her head still ached. She was definitely coming down with something. She sat up and stroked Maggie's head. "What happened?"

"They called me a slut."

"Who did?"

"Everyone. Tyrone was there, and also that guy from the first week, I can't remember his name. You know, you met him, he carried my tray."

"Kevin?"

Maggie sniffed. "Yeah. Tyrone got mad because I wouldn't go out with him again, and then Kevin joined in. Said I led them on."

Maggie's tears had dampened Nora's pajama top. "Well, you did sleep with them," Nora said, not unkindly.

"Yeah, but I never led them on. I just like sex, what's wrong with that? If I was a guy, no one would think twice."

It was true. Although Nora didn't agree with Maggie's promiscuity, she had to admit, what Maggie said was accurate. There was a double standard. No one batted an eye about a guy alley-catting around.

Maggie reached up to wipe her eyes and her hand errantly brushed Nora's breast. The sensation tingled erotically and Nora sucked in air raggedly. Maggie heard it, looked up inquiringly, saw the raw passion exploding in Nora's eyes.

"Nora?"

Nora groaned, tried to pull away, but Maggie held tight. "Don't leave me, Nora."

As Maggie tipped her face, the moonlight shone on her plump lips and Nora became fixated. She felt her face lowering, felt her own lips claiming Maggie's.

Maggie leaned into it, returning the kiss, opening her mouth and touching her tongue against Nora's. Nora tasted wine and the faintest hint of peaches. And more: Nora tasted *Maggie*. Everything that Maggie was – her beauty, her trust, her free spirit and boundless energy – it poured forth in that single taste. Nora's hand came up of its own violation, tentatively touching Maggie's breast and Maggie responded instantly. Nora knew what that nipple looked like – had seen it a hundred times when Maggie dressed, or strode around the room in her tiny panties and nothing else, or when she slept and kicked the covers off, leaving her naked body in full view of Nora's hungry eyes. Maggie groaned drunkenly and before Nora knew it, Maggie had slipped from her cat suit and stretched languidly in the moonlight, her body naked and warm and inviting. Maggie's fingers tangled in Nora's hair, bringing her face towards her breasts, guiding Nora's hands to the warmth between her legs.

Nora moaned. Sexual energy poured from her, freed after being denied an outlet for so long, electrifying her body.

Under the cover of darkness and the thin moonbeam flowing through the window, illuminating the handprint, Nora became Maggie Bench's newest lover.

CHAPTER FIFTEEN

'Each of us bears his own Hell' – Virgil

Nora fled the room early, dislodging Maggie's bare limbs which were wrapped around her like a choking vine.

What had she done?

Her face burned with the memory of it. She had to get out of here. Couldn't face Maggie now. Not ever.

Oh, the things they had done.

Her throat was raw and her head pounded. If anything, the pain had intensified. The Tylenol hadn't helped at all. She needed something specifically for sore throat and cold. Her nose was stuffed and her sinuses swollen and full.

Nora blindly reached for the first thing she could lay her hand on, some old jeans and a black sweater, and threw on a warm jacket. She didn't bother looking into her mirror, afraid to face what she might see. She stubbed her toe on something sharp and the pain exploded through her foot – the letter opener. Left lying carelessly on the floor. "For fuck's sake," Nora cursed, and Maggie stirred, but didn't awaken. The letter opener was potentially worth a hundred thousand dollars and Maggie had left it lying on the floor like a discarded candy wrapper. What was she thinking? It would get lost for sure. Nora slipped it into her back pocket for safe-keeping. She would encourage Maggie to get a safe deposit box, at the very least. The bedspread had fallen to uncover Maggie's creamy white back, and Nora took one last lingering glance, emotions conflicted. She had to get out of here. Had to think. Last night changed everything.

She walked hard for several blocks, slowing slightly as her breathing became labored and her symptoms increased. The cold air attacked her raw throat like razor blades. *Jesus, it felt like strep throat.* She couldn't afford to be sick right now, not with midterms looming.

And, she'd be contagious. Could have infected Maggie.

Tim Horton's beckoned and she joined the coffee crowd, lined up like sheep for their morning fix. She placed her order, her mind still frozen with panic, and ordered a half-dozen donuts. She took a table in the back corner, and systematically plowed through the donuts, getting to number four before her stomach registered the intake.

The coffee helped.

As the first drippings of caffeine met her central nervous system, Nora began to calm down and her pounding headache ebbed to a manageable level. Her throat was lubricated, still painful but not as bad. She'd stop into the pharmacy and pick up some medicine, even though she was already over budget for the week. It seemed as if everyone was staring at her. Like she had a neon-flashing scarlet letter plastered on her forehead.

'L' for Lesbian.

Lover.

Loser.

Was she a lesbian? She allowed her mind to retrace the night before and remember the pleasure she experienced, the passion so strong that even now the memory alone made her clitoris tingle and ached to be touched. To be suckled as Maggie had done.

And as she had done to Maggie's.
Oh, God.

**

Ashwin awoke and thought immediately of the poppy tea. What a disappointment that was. He'd followed the directions precisely. He had obviously been sold defective merchandise.

It hadn't helped his insomnia in the least. If anything, last night was the worst he'd experienced in weeks. When he finally achieved sleep, it was marred by vivid dreams and nightmares, jolting him awake. He'd dreamt of home – only this Pondicherry was vastly different than the one he'd grown up in, and as hard as he tried, he couldn't find his way home. When he finally did find it, his house was a battleground, filled with bloodied soldiers and Major-General Robert Ross demanding his father provide him with breakfast. He dreamed of Alec with his throat crushed by the tombstone, and the dream was so vivid, Ashwin awoke with heart pounding and profuse sweating, despite the cool temperature of his room. Alec had been trying to warn him but no sound came out of his ruined larynx.

Ashwin groaned. Midterms were coming up – it was imperative he get his sleep disorder under control. He resolved to return to the little Chinese shop and lodge a complaint with the proprietor.

**

Daniel stood in the study room, looking through the second floor window into the Quad. It was quiet now, not a single student lingered on its paths.

Alan Dressier.

Nora had called him a stalker.

He frowned. That was new information.

He would have to do some heavy thinking to see how that fit in and what it might mean.

**

Maggie woke feeling incredibly alive and refreshed. Sometimes after drinking too much, she'd feel lethargic but not this morning. She stretched languidly, momentarily surprised to see the room from a different orientation.

She was in Nora's bed.

She bit her lip and tried to think. Last night was a blur. She remembered taking Ashwin trick-or-treating, remembered his joy in soliciting free candy, lighting up like a little kid. That was nice – Ashwin seemed down lately and she'd hoped to elevate his mood. And, he'd looked so very handsome in his pirate suit – a Bollywood Johnny Depp. She remembered the parties, at least the first few. Then it got blurry.

Something had happened.

She'd been upset.

It was coming back to her. She looked around the room and groaned as the images flooded forth.

Shit. She'd drunkenly slept with Nora.

Fuck. Fuck. Fuck.

**

Feeling slightly queasy from the six donuts, Nora made her way down Spring Garden Road towards Pier 21. She popped into Shoppers Drug Mart and picked up some Benadryl. As she passed the public library at the bottom of the street, she went inside on a whim and settled in front of one of the public computers.

She input *Lila Rose.* Over three million hits.

She narrowed her search options by combining the name with other tags: *Halifax, student, King's,*

188

death. Better. She tried adding the date of Lila's demise: October 31, 1969.

Nora scrolled through them listlessly, looking for new information. *What was she searching for? A sudden answer?* Or was she just trying to keep her mind on Lila and off Maggie?

Both.

There was nothing new here. Lila Rose's obituary, a few links to newspaper reports.

It was a cold case, over forty years ago, in an era where social media didn't automatically afford a thousand-plus references to one's name.

In frustration, Nora input *Alan Dressier.* She was surprised to see an obituary notice. Was this the same Alan Dressier? A few more keystrokes. Yes, it could be – the age fit. Ah ha... here it was... Alan Dressier lived in Nova Scotia and died on October 24, 1969.

A full week before Lila Rose. No mention of how he died.

Were their deaths connected? It seemed odd to have two students from the same small university die within such a short period of time. Regardless, Nora sighed, she could rule out Alan Dressier as having anything to do with Lila Rose's death.

Maggie's skin in the moonlight. The taste of Maggie's hot skin on her tongue. Maggie's breast in her mouth. Nora pushed her chair away. She felt queasy and she knew it had little to do with the six donuts sloshing around in her belly. *How could she?* And, *what was Maggie doing now? Surely she'd be awake? Was she just as ashamed as Nora?*

Who was she kidding, Nora scoffed. Maggie Bench was never ashamed of anything.

Down to the waterfront now, walking with her head down on the cold autumn day, hands stuffed in her jacket pocket and refusing to meet anyone's eye. Into the museum now, at Pier 21, but a different face was at the admitting desk. Tom's shift wouldn't start for another two hours, his co-worker advised. She grudgingly coughed up six dollars, knowing it would eat even more into her budget, but she needed to get out of the cold, to sit for a while. To think.

**

"You cheated me," Ashwin said, his voice clipped.

The elderly Chinese man shushed him and looked around furtively. As he feared, this Indian boy was causing a scene. Other customers glanced over with interest.

"The product you sold me was defective." At the man's blank stare, Ashwin added, "The poppy seeds. I bought them from you yesterday – they were stale. I followed the directions exactly and the only thing I got was a nasty taste."

"Poppy seeds very healthy," the man stated. "Good source of fibre and minerals. Even antioxidant. Very popular now, I sell every day. Very delicious and calming."

"I think not," Ashwin countered. "Do I look calm?" He put the remainder of the seeds on the desk and demanded a refund.

"All sales final," the man said, narrowing his eyes.

"But this product is defective," Ashwin said, raising his voice louder. A part of him marvelled at his audacity: this new Ashwin was much more self-assured and forceful. "You will refund my money or I shall report you to the police."

Other customers were staring openly. The proprietor swallowed nervously. "Look, we come to agreement, make everyone happy. Maybe seeds were little bit stale; have had them for long time. They lose potency. I have new stock, in the back. I give you fresh seeds."

Ashwin thought about the foul taste. "I would prefer my money back, please."

"No refunds." The man pointed to a sign behind the counter. "Plus it says so on your receipt, all sales final. But new seeds are good, very potent. Will make you happy. I throw in a couple of pods, too. For free."

"Fine." The old-Ashwin was pleading with the new-Ashwin to take the offering. But the new-Ashwin wasn't quite ready to give in. "But if I find they are as weak as the first seeds, I will be back. Count on it."

"Maybe use more in your recipe?" the man suggested. "Grind the pod, too. Pod is stronger."

**

Maggie looked for Nora around campus, all the usual places, but she had seemingly vanished. She kept checking their room every twenty minutes or so, in case Nora returned. Maggie sighed. Her life would be so much easier if Nora just had a cell phone like everyone else. Nora said she didn't need one but Maggie disagreed. Everyone needed a cell phone – at the very least, it was common courtesy to be reachable.

As the morning stretched into afternoon, Maggie grew increasingly frustrated, and eventually, her frustration grew into anger. How dare Nora disappear like this, without even a note? Yes, the circumstance of last night was awkward, but even more reason to talk. Maggie penned a terse note, laid it on Nora's pillow where she was sure to see it, then threw on her sneakers and began to jog. A good run would help clear the cobwebs. She'd planned to run along the wooded trails of Point Pleasant Park, but as she passed by Rogers Drive, it made her think of Myrtle. It was an omen – she needed to see the spirit of Myrtle Rogers. She turned around and headed for the Hydrostone.

She was barely winded as she reached the park bench. Myrtle was sitting on it, waiting. Maggie sat beside her. "I've been trying to find you," Maggie said, and her breath came out in little puffs in the cold air. The weather wasn't hospitable enough for the park to be busy, but still, there were enough people around that Maggie kept her voice low.

Myrtle wrung her hands. "You are in danger," she said.

Maggie frowned. It was the last thing she expected to hear. "What? From who?"

"Your lover."

"Can you narrow that down a little?" Maggie thought of the angry voices of the boys at last night's party. They had brought to her attention there had been a lot of lovers lately.

"The one you were here with before."

"Tyrone?" Maggie asked. She remembered the love-making under the umbrella tree. "Myrtle, have you been spying on me again? You need to stop that, it's a disturbing habit."

Two young boys moved nearer, kicking a soccer ball. Myrtle began to fade. "Letter opener – danger... keep it hidden....beware of....seven..." Her apparition and voice faded before Maggie could make it out.

Maggie sat until she grew chilled, trying to ponder it out, willing Myrtle to return. *Seven.* What on earth did that mean?

They had just completed their seventh full week of school. Seven days to a week. Today was Sunday, the seventh day of the week. In numerology, seven was the *seeker*, where nothing is as it seems and reality often hides under illusion. Seven was also a *spiritual* number, and both seeker and spirit figured into the naming their group: the Spirit Seeker Society.

She thought some more. There was something else: pulling at the edge of her subconscious. The more she tried to fish for it, the more it stole away. And then it came all at once: *seven of swords*, the card the fortune teller had pulled. That fit – the letter opener was a sword of sorts, and there were seven jewels on it. What had it meant? She racked her brain, trying to remember but it was blank. She flipped open her phone and opened her browser, then Googled Tarot definitions.

The Seven of Swords warned of thievery and trickery.

Was it a warning about Nora? Maggie frowned. Hard to fathom, but if Nora Berkowitz could take advantage of Maggie's body – she was certainly capable of screwing Maggie financially.

The facts were there. Nora was broke, always bellyaching about how poor she was. Nora talked about selling the letter opener *ad nauseam*, making Maggie feel awkward and guilty. She thought about how the letter opener was always turning up in funny places. Nora joked that it was Lila Rose and blamed Maggie for being sloppy. But the truth was, Maggie was careful. She'd put it on her desk and then find it moved. Perhaps, one day, the letter opener would simply vanish and Nora would have her alibi – that Lila Rose was responsible for its disappearance.

Myrtle had said *lover*. Technically, Nora was her lover. Maggie's mouth turned downwards in distaste.

She did not have an appetite for females. Last night was a mistake – born of drunkenness and hurt. Maggie knew how Nora felt about her; she'd have to be a blind idiot not to see the thinly-veiled lingering glances that frequently came her way. Nora had taken advantage of her last night. Nora preyed on Maggie at her most vulnerable, and now, it was clear that Nora was planning to steal the letter opener.

**

By the time Tom started his shift, Nora had calmed down considerably. The medicine was helping and her throat felt better, although her head still pounded. And, so what if she and Maggie had one night of total madness – university was supposed to be a time of experimentation and exploration. It didn't mean they were lesbians. It just happened. She was fond of Maggie, loved her even. In a friendly way. Did that mean she wanted to jump Maggie's bones at the next available opportunity?

Maybe. She sighed. Last night had been... incredible. Beyond her wildest expectations. Would it be like that with a man, too? Would it be better? Nora closed her eyes and tried to imagine performing the same acts with Daniel. Her mouth parted and that is how Tom found her.

"Hey," he said. "Heard you were looking for me."

Nora started guiltily and blushed. *Get a grip*, she chastised herself. *No one can tell what you're thinking, just from looking at you.* Nora shifted a little. Her back had grown sore from sitting on the hard, acrylic bench. Her posture was terrible; she knew she had to do something about it. But, having grown freakishly tall by age thirteen, Nora had learned to diminish her height by stooping and it had become habit.

194

Tom was still talking. "Glad you're here. I have something you might find interesting. Got it from my sister." He pulled out a black and white photograph. Nora recognized the pretty features of Lila Rose. It was a crowd shot, but standing directly behind her was a young man with a hauntingly familiar face.

Daniel.

Tom pointed at Daniel. "That's Alan Dressier."

Nora's mouth went dry. The likeness was uncanny and she felt shivers run down her spine. How could it be? "Where did you get this?"

"My sister had it. I stayed with her last night – she doesn't like to be alone on Halloween, always worries about neighborhood kids getting up to shenanigans. We started reminiscing and I told her about your ghost search, and we got talking about Lila Rose. Linda had a box of old photographs so we sifted through them. She loved to take pictures back then. This was the only one of Lila Rose. But, look at that Alan fellow, see the way he's staring? I told you he was a stalker."

"May I borrow this?"

"Sure, keep it if you want. Hey, I was thinking about your ghost. Did a little research myself, have an idea for a ghost hunt for you."

But Nora wasn't listening. She was too busy staring at the photo. *It was Daniel.* But how could it be? This picture was almost half a century old. But there it was, in black and white. Same hairstyle, same handsome face. Same white tee with the short sleeves. She stood abruptly.

"Hey, where you going?" Tom asked.

"To show this to a friend. Thanks, Tom. You're a lifesaver."

**

Ashwin doubled the poppy seeds and poured in boiling water. He took a tiny sip. Still tasted weak and the color was light, not like the picture in the recipe. He ground up the two pods and placed them in the brew. He capped the thermos and let it steep.

This time, he wasn't leaving anything to chance. He would sample the tea himself, see what effect the stronger concoction had, and if he got even a mild buzz, he would bring it to the others. This time he would come prepared so he wouldn't look like an idiot.

He had called his father in India. There was an eight hour time difference. It was already night in India, but not so late his father would be in bed. The elder Pawar seemed pleased to hear from his son. Ashwin told him how his studies were progressing, and his father asked a few questions, and wondered how he was fitting in. "You will be very pleased, Papa. I even partook of an important North American tradition: Halloween. I dressed up like a pirate and went door to door, begging for candy. "

"Begging for candy? I am not certain I like the sound of that," his father said. "But I am overjoyed to hear you have made friends. You were always such a lonely child, Ashwin. It is important for you to take part of the world you live in. Be a leader, my son."

Ashwin told his father how cold the temperature was, and joked about the idiosyncrasies of Canadian food. "There is a very strange concoction they eat here," he said. "It is called *donair*, and it is truly disgusting. Shaved, pressed spiced beef with a sugar and garlic sauce – the locals love it, and there is a donair shop on every street."

His father laughed. "Try not to be judgemental, Ashwin. I am sure many of our dishes would seem strange to them."

"Alright, Papa."

By the time they finished talking, Ashwin checked the poppy tea. The color was darker. He sipped it – yes, still just as foul. He strained the tea and poured it carefully back into the thermos, keeping aside a large cup for himself. Would Maggie be in her room? He decided to take it over, see what she thought.

**

When Nora returned to King's, she realized she had no idea where to find Daniel. She didn't know which dorm building was his. He always came to their room, or met in the study room on the second floor of Prince Hall. Come to think of it, she'd never seen him anywhere else, aside from that one time in the beginning when he'd escorted her through the connecting tunnels.

On a small campus such as King's, she was forever running into familiar faces in the library, the cafeteria, the Wardroom, the Quad. Even if she didn't know names, she recognized faces. She frowned, thinking. She couldn't even remember seeing Daniel in the lecture hall. Ever.

She went to Administration and inquired what dorm room he was in. "Middle Bay, Room 217," the secretary answered. She pointed it out to Nora on the campus map. But when Nora knocked on the door, there was no answer. She looked at the picture again and kept knocking. *Boy, it looked like Daniel.* But the angle was skewed – the boy in the picture had his head turned, looking at Lila Rose.

Her persistent knocking roused a student from an adjoining room. "Jesus," he grumbled, "You're loud enough to wake the dead."

"Sorry," Nora said. "Looking for Daniel."

"O'Shea? He's playing football. Semi-final game. It's on right now, at Wickwire Field."

Of course. She'd forgotten. She could go back to her room and wait. *But what if Maggie was there?* Nora sighed. She reached into her pocket and took another swig of Benadryl. Looked like she was going to her first football game.

**

Maggie searched for the letter opener, first in her messy pile and then, when it wasn't there, in Nora's tidier belongings. The longer she looked, the more chaos she created. Soon, Nora's items were spewed about the room, her bed in shambles. The dorm room was small; there were only so many places an item could be. Maggie searched every nook and cranny, coming up empty.

The jeweled letter opener was not here. Only one person could have taken it.

Nora.

Myrtle was right.

CHAPTER SIXTEEN

'The blade itself incites to deeds of violence' – Homer

The football game was halfway through the third quarter. The stadium was full – many fans had painted their faces yellow and black. Everyone was cheering wildly. The scoreboard showed Home: 23 and Visitors: 21. Nora knew nothing about football but surmised Daniel's team was winning. She'd seen posters plastering both the Dalhousie and King's campuses advertising this match as the semi-final, with the winner advancing to the championship. The crowd was acting like Christ himself had risen from the grave. Nora could care less, and she squeezed in between two screaming maniacs. Something happened on the field – there was a great deal of yelling and cheering, and Nora thought this might be a good thing until she saw the visiting team's score increase by six. She studied the program given to her at the gate. It listed the players' names and numbers. There it was: Daniel O'Shea, number 57. She squinted at the field, trying to make out which player was Daniel. It was difficult to tell: they all looked exactly the same.

**

After an interminable amount of time, the football game ended. Nora did not understand the math of it. If a quarter was fifteen minutes in length, why did it take triple the amount of time to play? She was able to pick out Daniel's number on occasion. She didn't know enough about the game to tell if he was doing a decent job or not. The score remained close, and the Dalhousie Tigers won on the last play of the game, when their player kicked the football through the uprights. Pandemonium erupted and the fans flooded the field. Nora, jostled and poked, joined the tide of humanity and tried to find Daniel. For once, her freakish height was an advantage.

There he was, number 57. He still had his helmet on. *Crap, he was following the team off the field.* She elbowed her way through the crowd, earning a few dirty looks, and she grasped his elbow. "Daniel!"

He took off his helmet.

It wasn't Daniel.

"Yes?" He said, politely. Like Daniel, he had light brown hair and a similar build, but there the resemblance stopped. While Daniel was remarkably handsome, this boy was merely average. But his eyes were kind and he looked at her with patience.

"Sorry, I'm looking for Daniel O'Shea."

"I'm Daniel O'Shea."

"What? No, wait. I'm looking for a different Daniel O'Shea."

He frowned. "I'm the only Daniel on the team."

**

Nora walked slowly through the Dalhousie campus and crossed over to King's. Her mind was working furiously. Daniel had lied about being on the football team. Had taken someone else's name. Or was it all a silly mistake that could be laughed off?

She thought about Daniel. What did she really know about him?

It came to her she knew very little. While the others talked of their families and background, Daniel said nothing. She hadn't even known what dorm room he lived in. She'd never seen him off campus, only in the study room and her own dorm room. Oh, and in the tunnels.

200

Daniel had not come with them to Oak Island nor to her ill-fated birthday meal, citing football commitments. But, if he wasn't on the football team, where was he?

Daniel never talked of his past, never brought notebooks or a laptop. He was the first one to arrive at Society meetings, always dressed in the same white tee-shirt and jeans. Never put a jacket on when the rest of them were freezing. His tan hadn't faded. He shied away from physical contact. Yes, she could understand his unwillingness to touch her – she was a troll – but what guy refused Maggie's advances?

That didn't prove he was a ghost.

There were other clues. He smelled of lemons – ghosts were attracted to lemon scent. Or were they? It was something Daniel had said, she'd accepted it at face value; she would have to check.

Lights flickered when he was around. But, also sometimes when he wasn't. It was a very old building, so that was not a reliable clue.

And, then there was the photograph. The image of a student named Alan Dressier who died a week before Lila Rose – identical to Daniel, right down to the clothing. There had to be more pictures of Alan Dressier. Nora made a mental note to search the university database for old student records.

Was Daniel a ghost?

The thought was ridiculous. He was solid, flesh and blood. Not a partial image like Myrtle Rogers. *Or was he?* She had never touched him, he always pulled back. Perhaps, he had learned to manifest better than Myrtle.

She thought about Madam Denicci's statement: 'Someone is deceiving you'. *Was it Daniel?*

Nora couldn't believe she was even considering this. She must be off her rocker. She needed to talk to the others, to Maggie and Ashwin, to bounce the concept off them. *Well, not* Maggie, she thought, lips tightening. *Not quite yet.*

She found herself heading into the direction of the second floor study room in Prince Hall.

**

Ashwin knocked on the door. Maggie opened it, eyes wild and face flushed.

"Oh, my. What happened here? A tornado?"

"It's Nora's fault. She stole my letter opener. I can't find it anywhere."

Ashwin stepped carefully inside and set the thermos on the dresser. "Are you certain? That does not sound like Nora."

Maggie thought about last night. "Yeah, well, I'm starting to think we don't really know *what* Nora is capable of."

Ashwin surveyed the destruction. "Perhaps some fresh air, Maggie? To clear your head and calm you down?"

Maggie sniffed. "Okay. Thanks. You're a good friend, Ash. What's in the thermos?"

"Oh, I got fresh poppy seeds and made up a new batch of tea. I wanted your opinion."

Maggie opened the thermos and inhaled. She wrinkled her nose and then sifted through the mess until she located a mug. She poured a little of the dark liquid and frowned. "I don't know, Ashwin, this looks awfully strong."

"That is the point. Since we felt zero effect with the last batch, I decided to make a super brew – twice as strong. I even added ground poppy pods."

"Oh, Ash, no! You can't play around with this stuff, it could be lethal."

"Surely not? You said so yourself that it's all natural."

"Yes, but that doesn't mean it's not toxic if taken in large quantities. Even healthy things are bad for you if overdone. You could overdose on Vitamin C if the strength and quantity were enough."

His face fell. The new, daring-Ashwin was mortified.

Maggie softened, taking in his fallen face, and bit her lip. He looked truly despondent. "Oh, don't beat yourself up. C'mon, let's get that fresh air. And, something really fattening and delicious. I know, I'll take you to Julien's Bakery in the Hydrostone. Wait until you taste their croissants. They are, literally, to die for."

"Literally?" His mouth twitched.

"Okay, figuratively."

**

Nora poked her nose into the study room on the way back to her dorm. Sure enough, Daniel was there, standing by the window, gazing pensively at the Quad. The students were returning from the football game en masse, and the campus, so quiet a few minutes ago, was alive.

Daniel turned and studied Nora. "So, you discovered my secret."

She sat with a thump and kept her mouth shut, studying him. The silence stretched.

"Say something, Nora. Please."

She motioned for him to sit beside her, and when he did, she moved her hand slowly, placing it over his. He flinched but kept still.

Her hand passed through his as if it was air.

"How long have you been dead, Daniel?"

"A long time. But, you already knew that."

Nora licked her lips. "October 24, 1969?"

"Yes." He looked at her hand. It lay over his – or rather, where his should be.

"Tell me, Daniel. Please, help me understand."

His eyes met hers. "Are you afraid?"

"No."

Daniel closed his eyes momentarily. "Well, maybe you should be. I am a murderer, after all. I killed Lila Rose."

The lights were off in the room, but suddenly, they blared on, flickering erratically for a few moments before diminishing. A cold spell swept through the room, giving Nora goose bumps but she remained still. The curtains fluttered by the window, even though the window remained closed. "Yes, yes," Daniel said impatiently. "We know you're here, Lila. And yes, I admitted to killing you, albeit accidently. You know it was never my intention. I've been trying to tell you that for almost half a century, Lila."

The curtains stilled. *Run,* a voice in Nora's head urged. *Run!*

**

"I have decided," Ashwin told Maggie, "to return to India. I will finish this term – there are only six weeks left. Halifax is a lovely city, Maggie, but it is not for me."

"Will your father be angry?"

"Oh, he will be livid." Ashwin delicately bit into the croissant. Maggie was right: it was delicious.

"You look surprisingly calm," Maggie said, considering.

"Yes." Ashwin smiled. "I feel calmer than I have in months. This has been a great journey, Maggie, and I am grateful for meeting everyone. You, especially, have taught me something about being a free soul. This is *my* life and I must live it *my* way, even if it angers Papa." He took another bite of the croissant. "Alec taught me, through his death, that life is fleeting. Nora has taught me that kindness exists in the most unlikely places, and that light exists where you previously imagined darkness. And Daniel..."

"Yes?" she asked, when he would not finish.

Ashwin thought of the old caretaker. The realization about Daniel had come to him, suddenly, and he was surprised he had not seen it before. He would not share Daniel's secret with the girls. It was for them to discover. It was, Ashwin reflected, the true purpose of the Spirit Seeker Society.

"Ashwin, you are smiling like a Cheshire cat."

"Daniel has taught me that things are seldom as they seem. Our world is not black and white, as I had previously believed."

"Shades of grey?"

"More like all the colors of a rainbow. Our world exists as a vibrant palette. Even things, like the sky or the ocean, are different shades of the same color, depending on your perspective."

"A rainbow," Maggie clapped. "I like that." She reached over and held his hand, and Ashwin smiled.

Before, the contact would have disturbed him but now he felt the warmth that was Maggie flow into his fingertips. "I don't want you to leave, Ash. I'll miss you."

"Perhaps you will visit me in Pondicherry?"

Maggie grinned and the bakery lit up. "Yes, Ash, perhaps I will."

**

Nora produced the photograph of Alan Dressier. "Is it true? You were Lila's stalker?"

Daniel grimaced. "Not exactly. Yes, I was pestering Lila Rose, but you see, she had something of mine, something she refused to return. Let me see if I can explain."

The year was 1969. People wore bell bottoms and tie-dye shirts. In upstate New York, a half-million hippies rocked out at Woodstock. Across the United States, two million protesters marched against the Vietnam moratorium, and worldwide, 600 million people watched Apollo 11 land on the moon. Massive social change was taking place across the globe, yet Nova Scotia remained a sleepy hamlet, unchanging, and quietly going about its blue-collar, hard-working ways.

Alan Dressier and Lila Rose, along with two hundred other bright hopefuls, became first year students at King's. Alan and Lila had gone to the same small high school in Yarmouth, a town near the southernmost tip of Nova Scotia. They dated, briefly, but it didn't go past a few furtive kisses in the back row of the local cinema under the lone, unpatched-eye of John Wayne in *True Grit*. Lila liked Alan enough, he was easily the best looking boy in school – as handsome as Robert Redford, but he came from a large, poor family who lived on the outskirts of town and made their living on a farm. It didn't matter that Alan was intelligent, ambitious and certainly capable of, someday, a high-earning potential, Lila could not, and would never, get past the vision of his hillbilly family.

Lila did not come from wealth; her own father was a milkman, but, in her mind, it was many steps up from farming, and she lived in a proper house in town, with a picket fence and hanging baskets. Not on a rundown farm with pigs, sheep and squalling siblings running around the mud-soaked backyard.

Lila only visited once, and she quickly broke it off. After Lila's visit, Alan's grandmother found her wedding ring missing. She'd left it beside the sink in the farmhouse's only bathroom. Whether Lila took it was never proven, but the ring was not found, despite Alan's father's desperate effort to disconnect all the plumbing and check inside.

Alan was not terribly upset about being dumped. Truth was, Lila Rose was beautiful, but she was a tremendous snob, and her kisses were not worth the dullness of her conversation. He was furious, however, about the theft. He knew she took the ring, could see the guilt in her eyes, the fidgety way she squirmed and kept her hands in her pockets. She was supposed to stay the afternoon, they'd made plans to picnic at the lake with some other teens, but after her bathroom visit, she complained of an upset stomach and demanded to be taken home. The ring wasn't discovered missing until *after* her departure, and his grandmother was heartbroken. She'd lost her husband of fifty years only a few months before – the grief was raw and the missing ring served to ignite it.

Lila Rose avoided Alan all summer, but when university started, she was forced to see him every day. Alan was on full scholarship and held down a part-time campus job doing odd jobs to earn money for books and food. In his spare time, he committed himself to making a nuisance of himself to Lila Rose. He had promised his grandmother and his mother that he would get the ring. He trailed behind her, repeatedly asking for her to return it. "I know you took it, Lila. Just give it back, please, it's the right thing to do."

He sat behind her in lectures, at the cafeteria, and followed her around the Quad. Despite his constant badgering, she'd never respond, instead acting as if he didn't exist. Still, after almost two months of this, he felt she was starting to crack. He could see the strain on her face, the nervous tic, the way she was losing weight. Still, she ignored him. He had almost given up, realizing the futility of his actions, when she turned to him and snapped, "Fine. I'll give you the goddamn ring, it's a piece of worthless trash, anyway, just like you."

"You will?"

"Yeah, if it'll get you off my fucking back. Come to my room tonight."

"Boys aren't allowed in the girls' dorm."

"Do you want it or not?"

Alan knocked on her door promptly at seven. Lila greeted him with a sweet smile and an invite inside.

"No thanks," he said warily. "Just the ring, please."

"No, come inside, before someone sees you. Look, I'm sorry I took the ring. I didn't mean to, sometimes I just have to have things, I don't know why. My dad says it's a sickness. My mom says I'm like a crow, attracted to shiny things. Anyway, I was too embarrassed."

"Fine. I accept your apology. Where is the ring, please?"

"In a moment. I want us to be friends, again, Alan. People here aren't as nice as I'd hoped. No one even talks to me. Even my roommate is a drag." She looked at the ground.

She did look miserable.

208

When she looked back at him, her expression was calculating. "I'm afraid if I give you the ring, you'll turn me in, have me arrested. That can't happen, Alan. This place is my ticket out. I can't go back to Yarmouth, I just can't."

He clenched his jaw and tried to remain patient. "I won't. I promise. All I want is my grandmother's ring."

"Okay, but you have to do something for me, first. Something that will make us even – something illegal. That way, if you rat on me, I'll rat on you."

"Like what?"

She shrugged. "I don't know, steal something."

"No."

"Something, though. Something big enough that if you get caught, you could lose your scholarship."

"You are insane, Lila."

"Hey," she said, snapping her fingers. "I've got just the thing." She stood and began rummaging through her roommate's stuff. "Drugs. I'll take a photograph, to protect myself."

"I don't trust you, Lila. What's to stop you from taking the photo to the Dean?"

"And what's to stop you from going to the police? We'll both have to trust each other. Look, do you want your ring back or not? Do it my way, and I'll give you the photograph at the end of the year."

He considered. He didn't like the idea, but in a twisted way, he could see her logic. When the weather got worse, he would move inside from doing gardening to security, and he'd have access to the rooms. At that time, he could slip into her room and retrieve the photograph. He wouldn't turn her in – he didn't care about that. All he cared about was seeing the look on his grandmother's face when he went home at Christmas, with her ring on his little finger. "What do I have to take?"

"LSD. Just a hit."

"Okay." He'd tried it before, once. Along with marijuana – in 1969, drugs were prevalent even in small-town Canada. He didn't see what the fuss was – the pot was mildly enjoyable but the LSD was annoying. Alan liked to be in full control all the time, and the acid had left him wonky for hours. But he would do it for his grandmother.

Lila gave him the LSD, checked the flash on her camera, took the picture, and returned his ring.

He got back to his dorm room just as the drug took hold.

This wasn't like the last time.

Alan Dressier personally met all the demons he had learned about from Dante's nine circles of Hell. And, the last one took Alan with him. Alan Dressier died of an overdose on October 24, 1969, curled into a ball on the cold, bare floor of his dorm room floor. His roommate, away for the night, didn't discover him until the next morning. The rigor mortis had stiffened the muscles of his bronzed arms, and they bulged in death as he gripped his grandmother's ring in one hand.

Nora's mouth was dry. Her sore throat had returned, with a vengeance. She needed liquid, of any sort, to put out the fire. "Lila Rose killed you."

Daniel turned away. "It was accidental."

"Hold on," Nora said, her mind working overtime. "If you died a week before Lila Rose, how could you have killed her?"

"I frightened her to death."

CHAPTER SEVENTEEN

'The difficulty is not so great to die for a friend, as to find a friend worth dying for' – Homer

"Should I call you Daniel or Alan?" Nora asked, wiping invisible specks from her black sweater. Her thoughts were scattered. She was trying to make sense of everything.

"Daniel, please. That's who I am now." He hesitated for a moment, and Nora could barely hear him. "Nothing good ever came from being Alan Dressier."

"Okay, Daniel. *How* did you frighten Lila Rose to death?"

He raked his hand through his hair. "I didn't mean to, of course. For the first few days, after I died, I couldn't do much of anything. I was so confused, perhaps it was from the LSD in my system when I died – messed me up. I just drifted around, thinking it was part of the drug hallucination. When I finally realized I was dead, I had so many conflicting emotions. Sadness, anger, frustration. I would never be able continue my education, to live my life, to see my family again, to give back my grandmother's ring. Well, at least that part worked out okay, they found the ring gripped in my hand and returned it to my family with my personal effects. But my grandmother must have been very confused as to how I ended up with it. A few years later, she passed on, and I was finally able to explain it to her."

Nora was fascinated and momentarily forgot her dry throat. "Like, in Heaven?"

Daniel looked away. "Not exactly. More like the waiting room. I chose not to move on because I didn't feel finished here. Then, when I was ready, it was too late. I found I *couldn't* move on. I'm stuck here."

"And, so is Lila Rose?"

He nodded. "I think so. But apparently, she'll have as little to do with me in death as she had in life."

"Why do you want to see her so badly? You must hate her."

Daniel looked bashful. "I want to apologize, gain her forgiveness. I have the idea that if I can make amends with her, I may be able to move into the next realm. Be with my family again. Most have died now, except for my youngest siblings. I've been so lonely, Nora. You can't even imagine. Year after year, I've been wandering these halls. Each year, a new batch of students, so full of hope and excitement and intelligent ideas, and I can't reach any of them. No one ever notices me."

She licked her lips. They were as dry as her throat.

"But, why us? And how?"

"I'd learned to manifest almost right away. That's how I scared Lila Rose. I didn't mean to, just found myself drawn to her room. I think I was still trying to make sense of it all. That night, on Halloween, she not only saw me, but she heard me talk. She started screaming, totally freaked out. I tried to put my hands on her mouth to stop her, to calm her down. But my hands just went through her." He lifted his hand from the table and it drifted through Nora's. She felt nothing, perhaps the slightest chill. "Lila must have thought I was trying to strangle her. She put her own hands on her throat. Why? I asked that a million times. In her panic, did she think *my hands* were around her throat?" He shook his head. "When I realized what was happening, I started to back off, drifted above her. That made it worse. Her eyes grew frantic and her hands gripped tighter, and she stopped breathing. I think her heart just stopped."

"But the autopsy didn't show heart problems."

He shrugged. "Who knows? In 1969, technology was not what it is now. What really killed Lila Rose? I believe she died of fright. She knew she'd given me the LSD; was responsible – perhaps not intentionally, for my death. So, when she saw my ghost coming at her, it must have been an awful shock."

"And you've never spoken to her since?"

Daniel shook his head. "No. I know she's here, somewhere. I can sense her. But she won't show herself to me. Still afraid, maybe?"

"Are there other ghosts here?"

He smiled. "You'd be surprised."

"Alec?"

Daniel kept smiling but didn't say anything.

Nora tried another tactic. "Okay, tell me about how we fit into all of this. The Spirit Seeker Society."

**

"Should we get back?" Ashwin asked.

Maggie thought of the letter opener, about Nora. *About last night.* "No, not just yet. Do you mind, Ash?"

"Not at all." He smiled, realizing that here he was, in a foreign country, dressed like a white boy, enjoying coffee and croissants with a lovely coed, whom he could honestly categorize as his friend. Ashwin Pawar had assimilated. Perhaps his father wouldn't be so disappointed after all.

"Okay. How about a movie? There's an art film playing at the Oxford. How does that sound?"

"It sounds," Ashwin said, smiling widely, "wonderful."

**

"Okay," Nora said, drumming her fingers. "Tell me how this ghost thing works? I mean, you're solid-looking but Myrtle was only partially formed."

"I can manifest for short periods if I really concentrate, but only in certain areas. This room, for example, is a power source for me. I'm not sure why, the energy perhaps? And the residences, but only Cochrane Bay and Alexandra Hall. The cafeteria and Wardroom – I can only partially form. Too much noise, maybe? It helps if it's calm."

"And off campus?"

"No. The farther I go from here, the less I can materialize. By the time I get to the campus perimeter, I can't manifest at all."

Nora tried to take it in, to bend her mind around it. Maggie, no doubt, would grasp this instantly but for Nora it was a stretch. Daniel remained silent. "Would you mind?" she asked, holding out her hand.

He nodded permission and she slowly moved her hand towards him. This time, he didn't move back. Her hand went through his body as if he was air. She saw him grimace, slightly. "Does that hurt?"

"No. I can't feel anything. Ever."

"I don't understand, Daniel."

"Well, it's because I'm dead."

"No, I mean... the Spirit Seeker Society... was it just some joke to you?"

"No, of course not."

Nora's eyes narrowed. A number of snippy comments sprung to mind. "Help me understand, Daniel."

"As I said, I was very lonely. You have no idea what it's like to wander these halls, year after year, watching each new batch of students arrive and never being able to reach them. Oh, I tried, but it never worked. All I succeeded in doing was frightening them. So, this year, I decided to try something different. I'd hoped that if you got to know me, if I was another student, then you'd accept me." He saw her skeptical expression. "I'm explaining it all wrong. Don't be afraid, Nora. I won't hurt you."

"I'm not afraid, Daniel." Her voice was sharper than intended. She was caught between the urge to flee and the desire to learn everything. She forced her body to relax, allowing her shoulders to slump and, for once, uncaring of her awful posture. She studied him openly. Yes, this was the same Daniel she'd gotten to know. He looked completely solid. She put her hand out again and touched his chest, watching her fingers move through his torso as if he was nothing more than a hologram. Which, she supposed, he kind of was.

Daniel took her actions for encouragement. "It took me years to get the school officials to implement my society idea. I've been leaving hints and clues forever, but they were too daft to pick up on them."

"What kind of clues?"

"Whispering in ears, moving papers where they could find them – supporting literature. I can't take the credit for the original idea – I overheard it at a staff meeting. They were discussing ways to get non-resident students involved in campus life. Students who live off campus usually prefer to go home after the lectures finish, but many times, the true university experience happens out of the classroom. Even many resident students don't participate. The more introverted the student, the less likely he will join. Yet studies prove that students who are engaged in campus life are more likely to succeed, so the idea was proposed that mandatory involvement of an extracurricular activity be implemented, at least for a trial year. I was very excited – I might finally be able to make myself known."

"How did you choose *us*? How could you know *we* would create a society that searched for ghosts? And Alec..." her mouth went dry. "Did you have anything to do with his death? Did you kill Alec?"

"Whoa, hold on, that's a lot of questions. Of course I didn't kill Alec. That was a tragic accident. I would never hurt Alec. Why would I? He was my friend. I'd never hurt any of you." He put his hand out to her and it disappeared into her. "The selection was random. Anyone could have ended up in our group. I was just lucky, I guess. I couldn't ask for better friends. As for choosing our topic, I will admit to some manipulation. I guided the conversation toward the spirit realm. If you remember, Maggie wanted something health-oriented, and you suggested creating a society to help women in prison." He smiled a little. "I knew then that I would love you, Nora."

He said *love*. Nora flushed. "And Alec wanted beer-pong."

"Right. Quintessential Alec. When Ashwin mentioned a million souls passing through Pier 21, I saw the opening."

"But what if the subject of Spirits hadn't come up?"

"Oh, it would have, trust me, I'm very persuasive. Just a little nudge can totally turn the direction of a conversation. Not long after that, Maggie started talking about the ghost tour in frosh week."

"You said ghosts don't exist." It shot out like an accusation.

Daniel shrugged and allowed a small smile. "Well, I couldn't let the cat out of the bag, not right away, at least. You'd all have run from the room screaming. Look, I'm not proud of it, but yes, I directed the group to the idea of the Spirit Seeker Society. I thought if we were looking for ghosts, talking about them on a regular basis, everyone would become comfortable with the idea. Open to the possibilities. I didn't expect anyone to actually contact a Spirit, but figured if you did, that might pave the way for me. For you to *accept* me." He hesitated slightly. "Has it?"

"It's paved the way for me being supremely pissed. Were you ever planning to reveal yourself?"

He looked at his hands again and Nora felt he was hiding something.

"Out with it, Daniel."

He faltered and Nora watched as his form wavered. His edges became fuzzy, as if someone had taken an eraser and began to smudge. And, then, he was back to normal again. Well, if you could call it normal, she supposed.

"I knew you'd be the toughest nut to crack. If I can convince you, the others will follow."

"Is it your handprint on my window?"

He shook his head. "No, I swear. I think that's Lila."

"Huh. Did you scare those other girls into switching dorm rooms?"

He looked at her guardedly. "Maybe."

"Why?"

Now his face registered surprise. "I thought you knew, to be closer to Lila Rose."

"Not getting it here."

"I told you, if Lila forgives me, then maybe I can move on. That's my goal. Besides loneliness, I'm bored. I've been attending university for almost half a century now. Sure, the curriculum changes now and again, but mostly it's the same old stuff. The Classics never change."

"Try haunting the science wing instead, keep it fresh."

"Oh, that I could. But death, as in life, limits one's choices."

"Sorry. I didn't mean to be a smartass." A million questions flew through Nora's mind and she selected one randomly. "So, why pick Daniel O'Shea?"

"I needed to assume the identity of a real student, in case someone checked. I saw Daniel O'Shea in frosh week, chose the name because he resembled me a little bit. Same size, same coloring."

"I take it you're not on the football team?"

He shook his head and smiled ruefully. "That really threw me for a loop. I don't know the first thing about football, and Alec was so angry when he thought I took his spot. That was my mistake; I should have selected a student without commitments. But it was a blessing. It gave me an excuse not to leave the campus with you guys."

"Can you?" she asked. "Can you leave?"

"No, I'm stuck here. The farthest I can go is the campus limits. I've tried going to the Dalhousie campus but it's like hitting a glass wall. Even parts of the Quad are uncomfortable for me. Ghost physics, perhaps. Maybe we have to stay in our own area to avoid overcrowding." He saw her expression. "Just a theory. Didn't say I perfected it yet."

"No, but it would explain the difficulty in reaching Lila Rose. Perhaps she wants to materialize here but is unable. Maybe it's as difficult for her to come here as it is for you to leave."

"Hmm." He was silent. "That actually makes sense."

"What if Alec made the team? Then he'd meet the real Daniel O'Shea."

"Yeah." He hung his head. "Alec did make the team, as a reserve player. Well, would have, had I not interfered. A few days of whispering suggestions into the coach's ear made him select another player instead."

"That really stinks, Daniel. Alec was devastated."

"Yeah, I know. I wanted to make it up to him. Thought if I helped him with his studies, then at least he'd pass. He was a terrible student, you know. Alec never would have been able to juggle the demands of the football team and academics. But we're getting off track here. Nora, it's my fault that Alec died. I know I said I didn't have anything to do with it, but indirectly, I did. If I hadn't put you four together, he never would have died. Everything: the restaurant, the drinking, the graveyard... he wouldn't have been doing any of those things."

"I think it's fair to say he'd still have been drinking. Alec really liked to party."

He dipped his head. "Maybe, but without the other ingredients, he would have been fine. Just another drunken student acting stupidly."

Nora thought of herself after her birthday dinner, vomiting in the street. Of Maggie, stumbling in drunkenly last night. *Of what followed.* She swallowed heavily and the action was painful. "Don't blame yourself, Daniel. Things just happen, things get out of control." She shook her head to clear the mental images. "What next, Daniel? Where do we go from here?"

He tried to take her hands, but his fingers fell through, and he sat back with frustration. "I want to tell the others. Please, Nora. Will you help me?"

She nodded. "Okay. But I need to go now, Daniel. I need to process this."

To think about Daniel. And, Maggie.

Nora's head pounded relentlessly. She needed to lie down, to rest, to think. She needed to make things right with Maggie.

**

Just before the movie started, Ashwin became uncomfortably aware that Maggie was coming onto him. Her body language was rife – she was flirtier, touchier, gigglier. She was, Ashwin thought, like a cat in heat. He decided to put a stop to it at once.

"Maggie Bench, do not play your games with me." His voice was stern and he shook his finger in front of her, emulating his father.

"What do you mean?" She seemed genuinely perplexed.

"I will not have sex with you. Under no circumstances. We are friends."

She bit her lip and looked at the theater floor. "I wasn't suggesting you should."

"Yes, you were. Not with words, perhaps, but with your body."

Yes, she was. As the evening progressed, Maggie had started to think of Ashwin more as a potential lover and less as a friend. He was very charming, so self-contained and incredibly intelligent. He was so easy to talk to, Maggie felt as if she could tell him anything. *He was right, though.* She *had* been coming onto him. What the *hell* was she doing? This would totally screw up their friendship. "I'm sorry," she whispered. "I thought you found me attractive."

Ashwin smiled. "*Everyone* finds you attractive, Maggie. How can they not? You are truly beautiful." He reached for her hand and kissed it. "But it must never happen between us. Ever."

"Why not?" Maggie asked. "What's the big deal? It's only sex."

"No, Maggie Bench," Ashwin said, shaking his head. "It is not *only* sex. It is a magical gift between two souls who are meant to be together for eternity. By doing it with just anyone, the act is demeaned. It no longer becomes special."

Maggie tried one last time. "But, Ashwin, these are our fuck-years. Once you settle down, you won't be able to do this anymore."

"No, Maggie, you are truly mistaken. Once you settle down, with your one true love, *those* are your fuck-years. Otherwise, it has no more meaning than two dogs in the street. A pleasant diversion, perhaps, but with no value."

The theater dimmed and the movie trailers started. When Maggie would pull her hand away, Ashwin held it solidly. She pondered over his words. *He's right*, she thought. *He's absolutely right.*

**

Nora was mentally prepared to deal with Maggie – sort of – but not the disaster that greeted her as she opened the door. The dorm room was in shambles. Every item of clothing was dumped haphazardly; she could barely see the carpet. Even her area, usually immaculate, was trashed. Everything she owned lay strewn about, and her cubby door hung open, empty.

Nora groaned. *Obviously Hurricane Maggie had come to town.* She could NOT deal with this. Not now, with her head pounding and her throat so raw. Nothing was helping, no matter how much Tylenol and Benadryl she swallowed.

Nora methodically began picking things up. The action made her feel worse, and she felt like flinging herself on the bed and crying. She didn't even have the energy to go down the hall and get water from the vending machine. Then, she saw the thermos.

She unscrewed it and tentatively took a sniff. Ugh. It smelled foul – reminded Nora of her mother's herbal remedy for colds. Poppy tea- wasn't it? Hadn't Ashwin said it would help with pain? Help relax her? Help her see things differently? Nora sniffed again. If there was ever a day to see things differently, this was it. First, the sex business with Maggie, and now, Daniel's revelations.

'Don't drink it, her subconscious said, *it's not safe.' 'Oh, shut up,'* her mind answered, *'you're always such a worrywart. Where does it ever get you? Just make the pain stop and then we'll sort things out.'*

She tipped the thermos to her mouth and tentatively sipped.

She waited a few minutes, surveying the mess. The handprint on the window glowed, mocking her. *"Oh, piss off, Lila Rose,"* she muttered. *"I've had enough ghost-crap for one day."*

She could feel the effects of the tea almost immediately. Yes, it helped, the pain was receding. Emboldened, Nora pinched her nose and guzzled the rest of the tea.

And, then... she was floating. It was amazingly pleasant, heady even, until, abruptly, it wasn't.

The room started to spin out of control. She staggered onto her bed, lying on top of the strewn clothing and books. Something was digging into her back but it was too much effort to move. She groaned and shifted her body a little, trying to dislodge it, but it was still there. *The letter opener,* she thought groggily. *It's still in my back pocket and it's digging into my back.*

Within a few minutes, the poking in her back was replaced by new, immensely worse, sensations: her belly cramped with spasms and an overpowering nausea took hold, twisting her gut and intestines as if they were a dishrag. She wanted to vomit, but she held it in. *She would not puke all over her bed, all over her clothes.*

After awhile, came the monsters. Every misplaced item transformed into a devilish form, and they towered over her like gargoyles. Nora quaked with fear, covering her head. In one vision, her elderly father appeared – a hideous aberration – holding her birthday check aloft like an attacking flag. "Why didn't you cash this?" he derided. "Isn't it good enough for you, you ungrateful girl? You've changed, Nora. You used to be a good student and now your grades are no better than a B minus. You drink *alcohol,* and you have *sex* with *women.* You are a *lesbian,* Nora." He spat the word *lesbian* like a curse, and her embarrassment flooded her body until she was flush with shame. Her father's head was perched atop a goat body; his flesh the unholy burnt-umber of the Devil, his face alight with scales and horns sprouting from his head. Her father pointed and clucked, *"Poor decisions, Nora. You are no daughter of mine."*

Beside him was the figure of a ghostly girl – once pretty but now hideous as her skin stretched to reveal feral eyes and fanged teeth. When she spoke, it came in cackles, and Nora could swear she felt the foul spittle spray her face. "You are being deceived," the apparition crowed. "Don't trust anyone."

"Who are you?" Nora whispered, and the words felt like fire as they ravished her vocal chords, burning like a thousand litres of gasoline.

"I am Lila Rose." The ghost cackled again, then placed her spectral hands around Nora's beast-father's neck, squeezing, squeezing, until the blood-red skin turned black and his head exploded, raining a black-ichor over the dorm room.

A banging on the door.

"Shhhh," said Lila Rose, holding her face next to Nora's. "Don't. Trust. Anyone."

**

Like the perfect gentleman, Ashwin walked Maggie to her room and kissed her chastely on the cheek. She waited until he'd passed from view before using her key to open the door. She was feeling a little embarrassed, an emotion that was new and remarkably uncomfortable. She had no interest in seeing Nora with Ashwin as an audience. He had already seen into her soul enough for one day.

As she entered the room, she saw Nora immediately, curled on the bed. Nora's crazy-witch hair was splayed over the pillow and Maggie felt revulsion. Not at Nora, but at herself. When she spoke, her voice was rougher than normal, louder. "My letter opener, where is it?"

"Gooo-way," Nora slurred. "You're a monster. You're evil."

Maggie's mouth thinned and she stood there, hands on her hips. *Oh, great. Let's all dump on Maggie. First the boys last night, then Ashwin, now Nora. Yes, she might be a slut but she wasn't a monster.* "Where's my letter opener, Nora? Did you sell it?"

The letter opener, Nora thought. It is terribly important. But why? Why was this monster trying to take it from her? She had to keep it safe, keep it for Maggie. Nora fumbled, trying to locate it. Her fingers felt like fat sausages. She kept at it, watching as the monster came closer. "Go away. Isss mine."

"Give it to me, Nora. Stop fooling around." Maggie could see the glint of the jewels in Nora's hands. "Ah, ha. So you do have it. Give it to me."

"Never. Isss Maggie's"

Maggie reached forward, intending to grab it. Her foot caught in the terrible tangle of clothes on the floor and she fell forward, landing on Nora.

**

Nora felt the monster before she saw it, and she brought her hand up in defence, gripping the letter opener like a dagger, slashing at the monster. The first strike hit Maggie squarely in the neck, slicing her jugular, and she let out a desperate gurgle. Nora took this to be growling and struck again and again, slashing wildly.

When it was over, Maggie lay in a bloody heap on top of the clothes-strewn floor with seven deep stab wounds. Blood poured freely, in a river of red.

Nora lay back, exhausted. The room swirled and she congratulated herself for defeating the monster. She opened her eyes to make sure she had truly slain it, and in one awful, blinding moment of clarity, she saw Maggie. Her blond hair lay in a puddle of blood and ruined curls. Her eyes were frozen wide open, still beautiful, staring sightlessly at the window. *At the handprint,* Nora thought. And, protruding from Maggie's beautiful stomach, just above her diamond-pierced navel, was the hundred thousand dollar letter opener, buried to the jewel-encrusted hilt.

**

It took Nora the longest time to die. As the opiates from the poppy tea poisoned her, she slowly overdosed. Her body began shutting down. The goblins and monsters continued to torment her. Her father disappeared, and so had the Lila Rose creature. Now she saw Alec. He looked happy. He was wearing a football uniform. Not the black and yellow colors of the Dalhousie Tigers, but blue and white, with a cheetah on the front. *His high school uniform?* Or was this just yet another manifestation of the poppy tea-high?

Nora couldn't be sure.

"Don't worry," Alec said. "It's going to be okay. We'll all be together soon. You'll be happy, Nora. We'll be together forever."

Alec bent down to stroke her head and Nora tried to scream.

Or, at least she thought she was screaming. She wasn't sure if noise was coming out or if she was hallucinating this, too.

EPILOGUE

The deaths of Maggie Bench and Nora Berkowitz were deemed a murder-suicide. Stories abounded. "They were Satanists," someone suggested.

"Oh, I heard they were lesbians."

"Not the blond one – she liked guys. I mean, *really* liked guys."

"The tall one was really weird. I think she was a witch."

"Weren't they the ones looking for ghosts? Hey, maybe the ghosts killed them."

"Yeah, I used to live in that room. It was *definitely* haunted. That's why I moved out."

Speculation abounded and rumors were rife. The campus administration brought in a cleaning crew and sealed off the room for the remainder of the school year. No matter how desirable the corner unit was, they decreed it was not to be rented. At the end of the school year, they would review their options. Perhaps turn it into a utility room.

By Monday, campus life returned to normal and carried on as usual. The football team stopped celebrating their win and focused on next weekend's final. If they were to win, it would be the first time they took the championship title in the few short years Dalhousie had fielded a team.

The professors moved on from the Middle Ages to the Renaissance and Reformation years. The class started with a minute of silence for the fallen students, and then proceeded with the lesson, and by afternoon, everyone stopped focusing on the deaths and started digesting Shakespeare and Machiavelli.

The chapel offered extra counseling sessions for those who felt they needed it. The flag stood at half-mast, but the day was too bitter for all but the sturdiest of students to brave the outdoors.

**

Daniel, as always, was the first to arrive. He sat at the table in the second floor study room of Prince Hall and waited quietly. His face showed no emotion.

Alec entered next. He nodded to Daniel and took a seat, but remained silent. Alec unconsciously stroked the blue football jersey he was wearing.

Nora and Ashwin arrived together. They had been talking softly, and took seats side by side. Nora had not yet figured out how to manifest physically and was all air and glimmering motes. "Am I not any clearer?" she asked, crankily. "I've been trying really hard."

"Ten percent," Ashwin said. "But what I *can see* looks great. I have to say, Nora. Death becomes you."

"Is that some kind of sick joke?"

"No," Ashwin said. He was still not used to the idea that he was talking to a ghost. When she first appeared, it scared the bejesus out of him. At first he refused to listen, but with Daniel's help, Ashwin started to come around.

Alec began talking to Daniel earnestly. Alec had died weeks ago, had more time to get used to his ethereal body, and wanted to know everything. For every answer that Daniel gave, Alec had three more questions, and Daniel answered them patiently, endlessly.

"What I don't understand," Ashwin said, "is why everyone else is wearing what they died in, yet you, Alec, have on a football jersey. I know for a fact you were not wearing that the night you died."

Alec looked down. "I dunno. Daniel?"

Daniel said, "Beats me."

"Can you remember what you were thinking about when you died?" Ashwin said.

Alec frowned. Already the memories of his human life were receding. He thought back to the night when he was drunkenly running through the graveyard. "I remember hitting the tombstone," he said. "I was imagining playing football and that I was tackling it."

"Perhaps that is it," Ashwin said. He looked at the trio in fascination. After learning of the girls' deaths, Ashwin had begun preparations to leave immediately. His plan to stay until the end of the term evaporated. Then Nora appeared, sort of, and talked him out of it. At least, for now.

"Where is Maggie?" Ashwin asked.

"Late, of course," Nora stated. The annoyance in her voice came through at one hundred percent. While her visual manifestation was not perfected, there was nothing wrong with her voice. "Geez, even in death she can't be on time."

"Should we look for her?" Ashwin asked, finally.

Daniel looked out the window into the barren winterscape. A light snow had fallen and coated the ground. Everything was white and pure. "Let's give her a few more minutes."

Then Maggie floated in, wearing a thin sundress, looking as vibrant and beautiful in death as she had in life. The blood from the stab wounds bloomed like poppies on her dress, yet they were so uniform they simply appeared part of the pattern. Even her neck wound, the killing blow, was obscured by her ringlets, and didn't detract from her appearance. Nora wasn't sure whether to be annoyed or amused. It also irked her that Maggie had no trouble manifesting. While not as clear as Daniel, yet, she was nonetheless almost fully formed.

"Sorry," Maggie said. "There was the *cutest* boy in the Wardroom. I just couldn't help myself."

Daniel smiled back. "Okay, now that we're all here, I call to order first official meeting of the Spirit Seeker Society."

"First official meeting?" Nora interjected. "What were the other ones?"

"Rehearsal," said Daniel. "Now, let's get started. We have a lot of work to do."

-The End-

The Spirit Seeker Series continues in "Better Off Dead", now available.

BETTER OFF DEAD

(Book Two in The Spirit Seeker Series)

CHAPTER ONE

To journey you must first go out – The Oculatum

The fog manifested from the Halifax harbor, cloaking the city in gloom. The murkiness was a living entity – swirling, writhing, swallowing everything in its path and the evening sky grew grey with dampness. Nothing was untouched, every nook and cranny saturated until its victims could see no farther than their outstretched arm. It made even healthy lungs feel asthmatic and a clearing of throats could be heard sporadically.

Tiberius Ducasse swept back his dreadlocks and ignored the impulse to check over his shoulder. It was futile - he'd hear an adversary long before he saw him in this fog-soup. But this same paradox also protected him, and he slipped across Gottingen Street and through the sodden crevice between two derelict buildings undetected by all save a vagrant too inebriated to pay attention.

Every city has its skid road and Halifax was no exception. Gottingen Street traversed Halifax's North End, linking the Hydrostone neighborhood to the downtown core. In the dozen or so streets lined with pawn shops and boarded windows, Gottingen was home   to the city's downtrodden. Drug deals, prostitution and gang activity festered on Gottingen like an open sore. Despite a continued police presence, there was enough violence on a continual basis that most people avoided it. Even visiting

American Navy soldiers were forbidden to venture into the area after dark.

This was Ti's stomping ground. He'd grown up on these streets, raised by his Haitian grandmother, and he knew every misplaced brick, pothole and broken window. He knew which alleys to avoid when police were chasing – not because they were blocked, but because what lurked was infinitely more terrifying than the prospect of arrest.

Through the backside of the building, now, up three sets of twisting staircases that sprung forth from the bricks like corkscrews. He shared the top floor with his maternal grandmother. He didn't bother with the door – Grande-mère would have triple bolted it. Instead, he dislodged the loose window and shimmied in.

"Ah, Tibby." Grande-mère turned her head with a half smile. It was enough to show missing front teeth, and Ti crossed the room quickly and touched her hand. She squinted, trying to see him in the gloom but Ti knew she couldn't. Grande-mère was legally blind and her rheumy eyes left no doubt. She could make out his outline, at best. "Did you bring my chicken?"

"Yes," he answered, shrugging off his backpack. The pack bulged and squirmed and clucked as he laid it against her leg. "It better not have made a mess in there. Last time it took ages to get the shit stains out."

"Language, Tiberius!"

"Sorry. But it really was a stinky mess. This time I lined the bottom with newspaper so hopefully that will help." He flicked on a few lights. The small apartment was spotless. Grande-mère couldn't see much but she sure could clean. "Are you all set for tonight?"

"Yes. There will be fourteen in all. It'll be crowded but we'll make it work."

"Okay." He nodded. "Now remember, I can't stay for the ceremony. Maybe the first few minutes, and then I have to go."

"Yes," she sighed softly. "Frosh week. You explained it."

"Don't say it like that, Grande-mère," he tsked. "It's important to start right. I need to meet people, make connections. Especially since I'm not living on campus."

"You may leave after the *Priye Ginen,* not a moment sooner."

Ti nodded; there was no point arguing. He would stay for the opening prayer. He glanced at the table. It was set lavishly for the Spirits. Grande-mère had gone all out – tonight's ritual was important. Wooden statues, pictures, food, perfumes, and brightly colored flowers festooned the ancient wooden table. He wondered briefly where she had gotten the flowers, then dismissed the thought. Grande-mère had her ways. As always, a white candle stood alongside a glass of water. The Spirits would be well fêted tonight.

He adjusted one of the flowers slightly and Grande-mère's head swung sharply. "It looks nice," he said. "The Loa will be pleased."

Her wrinkled face softened. "Are you certain you won't stay?"

"No. And don't try to persuade me, Grande-mère. Your voodoo magic won't work on me. Not tonight."

She laughed, and for a moment sounded more girlish than elderly. "Don't be so sure, *mon cher.* Are you hungry? I left a plate for you in the kitchen. I'll warm it up."

Ti glanced at his backpack. The chicken was not happy and the backpack wiggled away from Grande-mère's leg. The poor creature was too stupid to realize its impeding fate but was trying to escape nonetheless and Ti admired it for the effort. Grande-mère toed it back into line and it stopped moving. "Thanks, Grande-mère, I'm starving. But don't get up; I'll heat it. You'll be busy enough tonight and you need to conserve your strength."

**

The University of King's College was teaming with nervous, excited frosh students and benevolent upperclassmen. The fog swirled through the inner courtyard of the Quad, dropping the temperature abruptly so that both males and females shivered in their summer attire.

"Only in Nova Scotia can the temperature drop this quickly, this fast," someone muttered and Abigail Lynn Soutter turned around to observe the speaker with interest.

"Really?" Abigail asked, bringing her shoulders forward in an effort to generate warmth. She wondered if she had time to dart into her dorm room and grab a sweater. "Is this usual?"

"The only thing usual about Halifax weather is there is no usual. You must be a come-from-away?"

"Calgary. Hi, I'm Abigail Soutter."

"Hey." The other girl nodded. "I'm Michelle Delaney, from Lower Sackville."

"Is that far away?"

"Nope. You really are a newbie, aren't you?"

Abigail started to answer when she noticed an absurdly tall boy standing behind Michelle and her mouth fell open slightly. He was broad shouldered, yet gangly, as if his body spent so much time growing

234

upwards it wasn't quite finished filling the midsection yet. He had dark hair that fell shaggily over his eyes and was long enough to brush the neckline of his AC/DC t-shirt. His narrow hips hugged low-slung tight black denims that had seen better days. One arm was heavily tattooed, the other arm less so, and colored ink played peek-a-boo along his collar bone and up one side of his neck. He wore a thick, studded leather wrist band, and Abigail noticed even his knuckles had letters tattooed on them, although she couldn't make them out.

But it was his face that mesmerized her. Eyebrow ring glinting above one arched brow, another on the side of his nose. Ears pierced abundantly and large black ear plugs in the lobes. And, topping it all, sanguinely mocking green eyes that watched her watching him.

He nodded, his mouth quirking slightly, and Abigail looked quickly at the ground, cheeks growing red.

"What dorm are you in?" Michelle was asking and Abigail started abruptly. She had completely forgotten the other girl.

"Um, Alexandra Hall."

"Cool. I'm on the other side, Chapel Bay. Jeez, it's hard to see in this fog. I wonder if they'll move things indoors?"

Abigail glanced over Michelle's shoulder again but the tall Goth boy had stepped back, and the fog obscured him molecule by molecule until he completely disappeared.

"Abby?"

"Abigail," she corrected automatically and shivered. "I'm freezing. Think anyone will notice if I grab a sweater?"

"Good idea. I'll come with."

They wove through the crowd. Abigail kept looking for the tall, dark haired boy with the tattoos and piercings and the incredible green eyes.

**

"Were we ever that fresh-faced and eager?" Nora asked.

"You were worse, actually," Daniel said, laughing, and Nora poked him in the ribs.

"It's hard to believe a whole year has passed," Alec said wistfully. "Frosh week, already."

"I skipped frosh week," Nora said. "It seemed frivolous."

"Oh, Nora," Maggie said. "You shouldn't have. Frosh week was a blast."

Nora looked down at the crowded Quad. The four of them were sitting on the Angel's Roost, the cupola and spire which sat high atop the roof of Prince Hall. "Yeah, I should have done a lot of things differently." Her lips thinned slightly. "I can't believe we've been dead for almost a year."

"Pfft," Daniel grinned. "Try almost fifty years over here."

"Time passes differently now," Nora said. "It seems like just yesterday since we... well, you know."

"Since you stabbed me to death and then overdosed?" Maggie supplied.

"Are you never going to let that go? Sheesh. It was an accident."

"I know," Maggie said, taking Nora's hand. "I was just teasing."

"Kind of a sick joke, if you ask me," Nora muttered.

"Well, I am *dead*. My sense of humor is supposed to be on the macabre side. Ghost protocol one-oh-one."

"I wonder if the football team will be decent this year?" Alec said to no one in particular. "They totally bit it in the championship game last season."

"*I wonder* if they will have mandatory societies again?" Nora said.

"Maybe." Daniel studied the crowd. The fog was growing thicker by the moment and it was becoming difficult to see the students. They would have to find a better vantage point. Perhaps the library steps? Or they could join the crowd. It wouldn't be like anyone could see them, even if they stood front and center and did the chicken dance. "The faculty likes to shake things up each year, keeping old traditions alive while injecting a little freshness."

"Hey," Maggie piped up. She'd been engrossed in watching some small drama below, like a vignette from a play. An attractive, conservatively dressed girl was eyeing a tall Goth boy like he was the Second Coming. Interesting. The boy smirked at her, she looked away and he melted into the crowd. It wasn't the same as being there, but it was almost like watching a movie from the front row. "I heard they're changing our old dorm room into a place for day students to go. There will be a couple of beds, so if someone needs to stay the night, they'll have a place to sleep."

"The *Day Bay*." Daniel nodded. "I heard that, too."

"Really," Nora sniffed, "that room is cursed. You'd think after three deaths they'd bolt the door and throw away the key."

"Well, they did remove the door. It's an open space now. Plus they gave it a fresh coat of paint."

"Like that'll help." The thought of students in her old room bothered Nora, although she couldn't say why. It wasn't like she'd gone there, since... the incident. Not even once. "Whatever are you looking at, Maggie? You're staring at the crowd like a tiger eyeing supper."

Maggie turned blue eyes on Nora, and Nora fought the urge to hold her breath. Even in death, Maggie had lost none of her beauty. "This fog's gotten so thick, I can't see anything. I'm going down for a better view."

"Why? Spy a good looking guy or something?"

"Sure," Maggie laughed. "There's all sorts of hotties in this bunch, but no, it's not that." She caught another glance of the conservative girl with her tidy ponytail, walking away from the crowd, towards Alex Hall. "Hey, catch you guys later, okay?"

Before Nora could answer, Maggie left her spot on the cupola and floated gracefully into the crowd.

**

Ben Bontel watched the ponytailed girl gawk at him, watched the way she'd taken it all in. His rocker clothes, his tats, his piercings. He waited for the freak-alert assessment to show in her eyes. Wait... wait for it... yep, there it was. That tiny little gasp of shock, the widened eyes, the quick lowering of her glance to the ground.

Always the same.

He wondered again if he'd made the right choice enrolling in this conservative, liberal arts college with a student body lower than most high schools.

He'd considered Montreal, Toronto, Vancouver... even New York, where an artistic person could express himself without being labeled an aberration. But King's was where he wanted to study. Let them gawk and judge; he would not let the moral majority influence his decision.

She was pretty. The thought caught him off guard.

He wasn't here to pickup fresh-faced college girls with shiny ponytails and wide-eyed curiosity. If Ben wanted to take a walk on the wild side, he'd hook up with someone of his own ilk. Someone whose soul was as dark and damaged as his own.

Ben stepped backwards and drifted away. Frosh week had been a mistake.

What to do? Too early to go home. Or was it? His roomies wouldn't be home and he'd have the place to himself. In theory, there were four guys sharing a two bedroom house within walking distance of campus. *House* was generous euphemism: it was no bigger than a shack and the number of residents tended to swell. On any given night extra bodies littered the living room with sleeping bags. The original four played poker to decide sleeping arrangements. The winner got the master bedroom. Ben was runner up, scoring the smaller but perfectly adequate second bedroom. He preferred it over the larger one; it had southern exposure and overlooked the tiny back garden instead of the street. The losers squabbled over the crawl space in the attic and the earthen floor basement. Neither was acceptable to Ben – there was no way he'd fit into the attic with his tall frame, and as for the basement... he shuddered.

The house was unlocked, and he was right – no one was home. The kitchen was a mess. Empty pizza boxes, beer bottles, soda cans, overflowing ashtrays. The garbage was spilling over, even though Ben emptied it earlier. *At least they were using the bin*, he thought. *That was an improvement.* Ben absently ran the sink faucet until the water ran hot and squirted a generous dollop of detergent.

His roommates were slobs. Ben had become the unofficial housekeeper. He made a mental note to gripe about it, to keep up appearances, but in reality, Ben didn't overly mind. He liked a clean house, found scrubbing and sweeping oddly therapeutic. It kept his hands busy and his mind free to wander.

When the kitchen was clean, he turned his attention to the living room. It stank of body odor and smoke. There wasn't much he could do. He wasn't about to go poking through others' belongings, even though these unpaid guests were technically squatting. But he opened the windows and the cool, foggy air immediately poured in. Ben breathed deeply. He could smell the sea. He straightened the cushions on the ugly green striped sofa, rebalanced a bong that was perilously close to falling off the coffee table and turned off the television. That was another thing; his roommates tended to leave the TV on, regardless if anyone was watching it or not. That stinking TV ran twenty-four-seven.

He needed to take a leak. The single bathroom, mercifully, was clean enough that he didn't have to do anything except hang up a tangle of wet towels someone abandoned in the corner.

He unlocked the door to his bedroom. The irony that the house remained unlocked at all times while his bedroom was bolted was not lost. Ben Bontel didn't own much, but what he did, he valued. He didn't trust his roommates and he certainly didn't trust the kaleidoscope of squatters.

He locked the door behind him and flipped on his desk lamp.

The room was furnished simply with second hand finds. His big splurge was the bed. At six-foot-three, a decent bed was paramount. For now, he'd propped the mattress and box spring on bricks and that seemed to be working okay. He'd learned recently the margin between cheap percale and decent linen meant a world of difference in gaining a decent sleep, so he'd purchased only one set of sheets, but they were quality. He'd found a great old wooden desk at a yard sale for twenty bucks, and talked them into throwing in the chair for free. He'd scrounged shelving from behind Wal-Mart – new but damaged on one corner. A small bar fridge stood in the corner, traded from another student for Ben's leather jacket. He'd hated to part with it, but damn if he was going to share his food with the outside vultures. Three days of watching his groceries disappear cured him of the notion his roomies would respect the *'everyone has his own shelf'* rule.

He still needed to find a dresser. For now, his clothing remained stacked neatly on the bottom shelf. He'd been trying to nail down a dresser since he moved in a few weeks ago, but it eluded him.

Aside from the bed, his only extravagances were his books, an old guitar, and a couple of sculptures. Half the books were required texts for the Foundation Year at King's. The other half were old favorites he couldn't bear to part with when he left home.

The sculptures, in a variety of mediums – clay, metal, driftwood or a combination of all three, decorated the far wall. They were breathtaking and manic and confusing and eclectic. They were exquisitely tormented expressions of art better suited in a museum or gallery. Ben turned his back on them. These were completed so they no longer held interest. He picked up one that was half formed and idly began running his fingers over it.

It was only nine o'clock. He could finish working on this one, or start another. Or, he could stretch out on his comfortable bed, while the sweet Atlantic fog rolled in like a thundercloud, and unlock the amazing mysteries of these new text books. He flexed his tattooed arms and weighed his decision. And finally, he grinned. A beautiful, soulful smile Ben kept hidden from the world.

For the first time in his life, Ben Bontel felt like he was the master of his own destiny. For the first time, he could do *whatever* he wanted.

Better Off Dead, available in print & Kindle

Also by S. Kodejs:

About the Author:

S. Kodejs was born in Vancouver, British Columbia and currently lives in Halifax, Nova Scotia. She loves writing scary fiction with a socially conscious edge. "My best compliment is when my readers say they need to keep the light on after reading my work. I practise reading my material on my husband and three sons. It's hard to creep them out, so when I do, I know the material is working. My goal is to craft stories that give goosebumps while making the reader think, 'Hmm... What if that really happened?'" Hobbies include a love for travel, cheering on St Mary's University soccer and football teams, and hiking with her dog, Bru.

23395102R00143

Made in the USA
Charleston, SC
19 October 2013